I0518903

Nonlocal Science Fiction

September 2015 - Issue #3

Daniel J. Dombrowski, editor

Guest Editors:
Dave Dombrowski
Ariel Hawkins
Noah Purdy

ISBN 978-0-9961723-6-3

Published by:
33rd Street Digital Press, LLC
P.O. Box 9294
Erie, Pa. 16505

www.thirtythirdstreet.com
nonlocal@thirtythirdstreet.com

Table of Contents

Introducing the
Fantastical Fiction Feature
on NonlocalSciFi.com

100% FREE short stories that you can read any time on NonlocalSciFi.com.

"What's In A Name?"
by Nicholas C. Rossis

"Dumped From Spinning Ship"
by John Grey

"Perspectives"
by David Reinersmann

Plus many more! Only on NonlocalSciFi.com.

Letter from the Editor

Dear Reader,

If this is your first time reading an issue of *Nonlocal Science Fiction*, welcome. If you've done this dance with us before, we're happy and extremely grateful to have you back. I wish I could say that putting one of these things together has gotten easier, but the fact is that we've poured just as much, if not more, of ourselves into this issue than in those that have come before it.

Inside this issue, you will find seven wonderfully imaginative short stories, the third chapter of Thad Kanupp's increasingly astounding serial *Deal Gone Bad*, and our first-ever poem, a sweet set of verses by John Grey with the title "A Clone Writes".

The poem is not the only first we have to share with you. On our website, NonlocalSciFi.com, we have begun posting short stories in a series we are calling the Fantastical Fiction Feature. All of the stories are free to read and will remain that way until the Internet crumbles and turns to dust.

You'll recognize quite a few authors who have graced the pages of this magazine, but you'll also notice a good number that you've never heard of before. The FFF is all about seeking out and recognizing new, talented writers who have never found an outlet for their work. The goal of *Nonlocal* from the beginning has been to expand the science fiction genre by bringing lone independent authors in from the cold and helping them find readers. We like to think we're doing a pretty good job of that, so far.

Keep checking the website and consider signing up for our email newsletter to hear about new free stories and special discounts on the magazine before anyone else. We are thrilled you've joined our little cabal by getting your hands on this issue, and we hope you stick around to see what else we have planned for the future.

All The Best,

Daniel J. Dombrowski, editor

THERE'S A SMALL CHILD IN US
WHO ONLY CARES ABOUT THE PICTURES

COVER DESIGN BY
BIOBLOSSOMCREATIVE.COM

The Unborn

Written By
Cristóbal Matibag

Seeing the directors wearing the little visors always made Corbett grin. He'd watched as they'd put them on and studied the different faces they made as the viewing glass clouded. He could smirk unobserved while they adjusted to the darkness, squirming or nodding as the hazy lights and amorphous figures began to break it. After a few minutes, he slid the white-noise fader toward him so they could hear his voice.

"What you're seeing, gentlemen, is exactly what your clients will see all the time," he said. "And that rushing sound you hear is the constant, personalized backing track. You're each generating your own right now. To be precise, it's the sound of your own bloodstream, just amplified and modulated; it's more or less what you hear when you cup your ear or stick it in a conch shell. Reach up to that sensor—the one just beneath your ear and behind your jaw. That's what's picking it up. Listen closely, and you might be able to hear how it's been blended with samples of human speech. Don't worry if you can't, though. They're practically subsonic."

The men's right hands rose in unison.

"You can see—and hear—how a phrase like 'sensory deprivation' doesn't do justice to the technology. The engineers' ideal was to recreate a very specific environment, one that all of us have lived in but none of us recall: the maternal womb. You'll be able to see how well they've realized it when we have our walk through the tiers."

Exhaling, he slid the fader back to the default setting. Corbett was glad he'd decided not to use a visor himself. Going without one let him keep a firmer hold on his sales pitch. They'd taken this one so well that he could speak of the tour without any hint of presumption. He was sure they'd be there.

*   *   *

As he led the group from the elevator, Corbett reached the second-to-last part of his standard tour patter.

"You've all heard about the outcry we dealt with when the first system was installed. They called it 'cruel and unusual.' They said it was callous to let their bodies waste in these units. But what do free people use their bodies for now? Walking from their apartments to the maglev, and from the maglev to work. And that's if they're part of that hallowed group that *gets* to work. You know that none of these guys are scientists, technicians, artists. They're a long way from being corporate board members like you. If they ever worked at all, it was to repair some kind of AI-equipped machine whose functional intelligence—its actual capacity to learn and iterate itself—vastly exceeded theirs."

He waited for their collective chuckle to wane.

"The point is, neither their minds nor their bodies were significantly more engaged then they are now." He gestured to the clients reposed around them like jumpsuited mummies. They seemed to stir in support of his point.

"The other big outcry was over the immersive environment. It was, by definition, infantilizing. But what kind of environment should they have had? What would you call their 'natural' environment?"

One of the board members, a debauched-looking B-school type, broke in.

"I don't get why you don't make it, like, a perpetual kind of fantasy for them. Maybe a fantasyland for violent felons. Something out of a 21st-century console game. They could die in Mexican standoffs, t-bone each other's cars, have orgies, overdose and come back—"

Corbett parried with his standard rebuttal. "There were some graduate students at a few tech schools that ran an environment like that. Not just that, either. There was a whole VR-engineering program that tried to develop different wish-fulfillment scenarios along the same lines. Project Paradise was what they called it.

"But they had a problem. This wasn't for the consumer market. The objective was to obviate the, uh, client's awareness of his own confinement. They wanted to relieve him from being conscious of the way he was crammed cheek-to-jowl with a bunch of guys like him. And when they beta tested the Paradise stuff, the subjects got restless. They recognized the patterns too quickly. They got bored. They felt trapped. Then they would get despondent or violent, generally. As far as I know, nobody, not even Dante or Milton, has ever conjured a wholly appealing vision of paradise."

His interlocutor fell silent, so Corbett moved on to his final topic.

"We always get groups that ask why the system's called 'AVE.' To answer that, we have to go back quite a few decades, to the middle of the last century. That was when they first started using systems like this on a broad scale. I'll bet you can't guess who they used it on first."

One of the younger members spoke up. "Old people. People with Alzheimer's. Or maybe dementia? I'd bet around the time they got too numerous to keep in the old kind of care facility."

"That's a fair guess," Corbett said. "But it's actually way off. Anyone else?"

He let them wait in silence for a few beats before pressing on.

"Poultry. They used it on chickens that laid eggs. Today they're kind of a…specialty product, but back then, they sold by the billions. And producers housed laying hens in these huge battery cages. Talk about a rough life! The poor things spent their lives in wire boxes that were hardly bigger than they were. Sometimes they couldn't stand up or spread their wings all the way. Sometimes their feet actually grew *around* the wires of the cage. Imagine what that would be like."

The directors craned their necks to take in the surrounding tiers, mentally replacing the visored, intubated occupants with suffering hens.

"Then, in 2052, a coder and a computer engineer, Ahmad Elhai and Liao Xiao, perfected this immersive, totally virtual environment that replicated the sort of outdoor expanse a free-range chicken lived in. The chickens had these little headsets—the precursor to the standard AVE visor."

The kid spoke again. "Okay, but how did the chickens influence the name?"

"There's a double meaning," Corbett said. "Like it says on the website, the letters in 'AVE' stand for 'Autogenerated Virtual Environment.' But the word 'ave' also means 'bird' in Latin. *Aah-vay*. It's our little nod to Elhai and Xiao and to all those happy, egg-laying hens who thought they were running free."

Corbett's audience gave a satisfied murmur, which was drowned by the tiers' electromagnetic hum.

*   *   *

That evening, as he stood in the packed 6:15 maglev, Corbett congratulated himself. He'd given a decent pitch, though it had been rawer and more candid than his usual one. When he remembered parts of it, he almost sounded bitter to himself. Even if he had been a little off-key, he didn't think it would make a difference. He knew that the chairman was desperate to keep up with all the latest advances in corrections.

Fruitful as it had been, the day's work had drained him. No matter how many sales he closed, no matter how many awards or bonuses or package trips he won, Corbett couldn't shake the jittery feeling he got while giving the tours. It was, as every rep learned, the stage in a deal that made or broke it. Taking (as he so nearly had) the wrong tone or hitting the group with too much of the history behind AVE, you could easily lay waste to months of calls and meetings. Accordingly, the team at UTech regarded Corbett, the sales leader for three straight years, with a mixture of envy and awe. But they didn't know how much effort it was costing him lately to project the usual calm.

Eva was waiting for him at the obstetrician's. He guessed she'd been glad to get out of their little apartment, but it had probably been a rough trek to Dr. Alt's building, especially since her feet were so swollen these days. Corbett reflected on the ache in his own feet and imagined Eva standing all the way to the high-rise where Alt practiced.

Eva's pregnancy was the culmination of a year's worth of doctor's visits, tests, and invasive procedures—most of them borne by Eva in his absence. Her endometriosis and the extensive scars it left had made most of the specialists they consulted doubt her ability to conceive. He'd wanted to go to more doctors' visits with her, but he could rarely shift his meetings or calls to accommodate them.

Perhaps it was better that way. He'd always been ambivalent about kids. It wasn't that he disliked them. In fact, when a mother at a family get-together or a company function brought her baby over, he was usually glad. He felt a secret pride in his ability to divert or soothe them, and he was charmed by odd expressions and habits of speech that the newly verbal ones came up with.

At the same time, he'd never been able to answer the grave internal voice that told him it was reckless to have children. For years, he'd been reading articles that said Earth had exceeded its carrying capacity for human life. Right up until the week before the final in vitro attempt, he'd asked Eva if it was really justifiable—defensible, even—to create a new human life.

When they argued, he'd always raised the topic of resource exhaustion and how the worldwide fear of it had spurred such unbelievable changes. They'd lived through things they never could have imagined when they were kids in Piscataway.

Corbett would always run through the same general set of talking points, as though he were giving some sort of reverse sales pitch. He didn't have to mention the way prisons, even back when people still used that term, burgeoned with inmates. She'd known about the riots and the breakouts. She'd lived through the successive crime waves that followed the release of all those felons in Essex County—a microcosm of what had happened, and gone on happening, around the world. Why no one had been able to reinstate the death penalty was beyond him.

Corbett could draw evidence from plenty of other corners. His dad had been president of a leading feed-additives company, before livestock production had dwindled to the point of being an economic afterthought. It was a casualty of the global shift toward less input-intensive sources of food, which droughts, livestock epidemics, and popular pressure had essentially forced.

Before he and Eva had even been born, private, gasoline-powered cars had been junked in favor of the desperately crowded magnetic rails they had to ride everywhere.

Euthanasia, once so contentious and controversial, was now established as a medical specialty; both his dad and Eva's great-aunt had wanted to go to the same clinic for theirs. As it happened, the place was too heavily booked for either of them to get on the waiting list.

Right before Eva fled into the bedroom or out the door, Corbett would usually say something about not wanting to crowd the planet any further.

Yet after all that, he'd still given in to her. He had a host of reasons, some of which he'd kept to himself. He hated the times when she'd stop talking to him or evade his touch. She'd said since the day he was promoted that they'd be able to afford a child without changing their standard of living, and he couldn't pretend otherwise—not even after she left her job with Vertical Realty.

And despite all the evidence he piled at her feet, there were times when he wished for a baby too.

*   *   *

The doctor's face, usually so jovial, was grim when Corbett joined him and Eva in the consulting room. Alt was watching the screen of his palm-sized ultrasound device.

"How's she looking?" Corbett asked.

Alt paused a long time before asking, "Your wife or your daughter?"

For the first time, Corbett wondered if he was stalling. He hadn't allowed himself to think much about the child his wife was carrying, though there was plenty to think about.

She wasn't getting nourishment from the placenta. There was something wrong, Alt said, with the umbilical cord.

Corbett squinted as he turned his gaze from Alt to the screen on his office wall.

"Why is she touching her face like that?" Corbett said. The way she was placing her hand over her nose and mouth made him wonder if something else was going wrong.

"*That* is the last thing we need to worry about right now." Alt said, still looking at his own screen.

Corbett remembered how once he'd seen an inmate (he'd never get used to calling them "clients") do the same thing. He'd stopped in the midst of a series of isometric self-clutching exercises, which techs guided the inmates through to guard their muscles against total atrophy.

As the heat from the man's cupped breath had clouded his visor, Corbett had wished he could take out his cell camera. He'd never seen an inmate look so vulnerable.

Alt broke his reverie with distressing news. He'd been talking for a few minutes, but only now did Corbett hear him.

"We'll have to do an emergency caesarian," he said, looking at Eva.

"Is she viable?" Eva said. "I'm hardly in my second trimester."

"She will be. But she'll have to spend at least a couple months in the NICU downtown. Her lungs haven't had time to develop."

"What?" Eva whispered.

"The Neo-natal Intensive Care Unit," Alt said, reaching for a phone. "We're going to deliver her. Stay there; I'm having Lynette prepare the birthing room."

*   *   *

Corbett still had his daughter in mind as he walked the tiers with Peter Cilious. She was still in the NICU, where he'd taken to spending his nights with Eva. Together, they watched their Madeline writhe beneath the curved plastic cover of her incubator. She'd been scarcely more than a pound at birth.

Peter, now the chairman of the Panopticon board of directors, had bought the earliest AVE units. He usually consulted UTech before making a new round

11

of upgrades. But today, he'd brought Peter in to discuss a bigger project: the old supermax prison he was planning to retrofit with AVEs.

Corbett wished he was awake enough to give Peter his full attention. He knew his best client had a big proposal to drop on him. He'd contracted a few different outside firms to help him develop some new design ideas for the facility. Surely they'd be in keeping with Peter's maverick image.

Peter's ceaseless drive to expand and change made some people in the industry wary. It was he who'd coined phrases like "the penal revolution," and later "the post-prison era." In a way, Corbett admired the way he balanced profit with an apparently progressive ethos. At the same time, he didn't like Peter's obsessive focus on meeting the "per-share earnings target" he set every year at the Panopticon shareholders' meeting. He was too tired to remember precisely what that phrase meant. All it meant to him at the moment was that Peter was looking to cut as many salaried positions as he could. He had to deliver those earnings. But how was he planning to do it this time? Before Corbett could pose his question to Peter, he sensed the latter pulling his arm in the direction of the Screensitters' Lair.

The Screensitters' Lair was their private name for the control center where various technicians sat in front of their monitor banks, making sure the AVE system stayed in working order. There was one who tracked nothing but the inmates feeding tubes and catheters; another watched vital signs like heart rate, O_2 saturation, and temperature; another tweaked the mix of drugs that kept the inmates in a blissful state of semi-consciousness; yet another called forth the sanitizing mist that cleansed both the bodies of the inmates and the molded plastic casing that covered their individual units. Surprisingly few of them were needed to watch a population of 3,000. They manned their stations in poses of relative lassitude. They seldom had to override the command sequences that the AI was programmed to run through.

The hum in the hot, cramped room kept the team from hearing what Peter was telling Corbett.

"I know no one's dared to try it," he said, "but I want to see if we can go off-site with the screensitters. I'm looking to go way off-site, actually. Overseas."

Peter waited for Corbett, to reply, but his friend only stared at him.

"It's been possible for years, but no one wants to take the public-relations hit that outsourcing these guys would invite. We're looking at a spot in the Philippines."

Not wishing to seem obtuse, Corbett improvised some objections. "What happens if there's a typhoon or something? What if your remote lair loses its connection or if there's some kind of delay in the data stream from the sensors? Aren't you worried about problems like that?"

"Hardly. They'll only be there to back up this new AI system that's in the pipeline. If we've got it right—and I think we do—we can completely phase out the overseas screensitters within the next five years or so. Our goal is to have zero human inputs."

Corbett looked at the men craning innocently over their monitors.

"Would you implement that here, too?"

"Everywhere I could."

"Your human resources department is going to hate you."

"Yeah, but the major shareholders won't."

"That's for sure," Corbett said.

*   *   *

It had hurt him watching Madeline try to breathe. Her alveoli, those tiny sacs that traded oxygen for carbon dioxide, were too sparse, as were the cilia that should have been clearing away mucus. After giving her a course of surfactants to break her phlegm up, they put her on an oscillator, a sort of vibrating table designed to loosen her congestion. As he watched her tremble, he wondered if she was conscious enough to feel anything.

Eva hadn't slept for two days running. Corbett had only gotten a few fitful hours. Their vigil was entering its third month. All the while, UTech's various departments were working in concert to install the system his newest clients had signed the contract for three months ago. He was supposed to show up in Trenton to check out the site tomorrow. And before that, he had to call on Peter to see the model of the new individual AVE units. He wondered how he'd keep himself together for the visits.

"You know I have to go, right?"

"Yeah." Eva didn't look at him.

"Will you be okay?"

"I'll be fine. I'll call you if anything happens to Maddy."

*   *   *

In Peter's office, Corbett had watched as the hologram of the new AVE units rendered. After a minute or so, he saw the image of two inmates. One lay strapped to his unit upside down, facing an identical, right-side-up companion at a distance of mere inches. The head of one occupied the hollow where the shins and feet of the other met.

"You must have inverted part of this and superimposed it on the other part," Corbett said. "You've got yin and yang here."

"That's the idea."

"You ought to get a new stock response, Peter."

"No, it really is." Peter flashed a devious smile, one that made him look a bit like that 20th-century magnate Richard Branson. We can't build new facilities fast enough to house these guys. We're not going to kill them. We're too civilized for that. This setup is the future."

"They haven't got space to do the isometric routine. And how do you plan to clean them?"

"We can stimulate their muscles with patterns of electrical pulses that simulate bearing a load. And we've got these neat little nanobots that cover them head to toe and suck all the grime away. You should see it. They gleam. They're like a swarm of shiny white maggots that only lick the flesh. They leave the client practically sterile."

"You wouldn't happen to have prototypes here, would you? I haven't showered in a couple of days."

"I've got a shower stall in the bathroom over there. Why don't you hop in and get back to the NICU before you see my moribund competitors?"

Seconds later, as the hot water ran down his body, Corbett imagined they were Cilious's high-tech maggots, licking painlessly at his flesh until nothing remained.

*   *   *

Before he got past the gates of the new facility, Corbett was sure he should have stayed at the hospital. He felt sick. In the NICU, he'd learned that the course of IV steroids they'd pushed to get Maddy's lungs growing could cause cerebral palsy and other neurological problems. He'd also had to weigh the pros and cons of installing a gastrotube for nourishment. She was struggling to feed from the other tubes—first through the mouth, and then through the nose—that they'd tried so far.

As he climbed to the highest tier, trying to get a better view of the whole containment area, he wondered what kind of life his girl would have to look forward to. Would her brain be well enough developed for her to do a scholastic program? Would she test well enough to get a place in one of the dozen or so career-track universities in the world? Or would she have to while her life away the way ninety percent of humanity did, trying to string together enough momentary diversions to last a lifetime? He had an unceasing suspicion that her life, such as it was, would be subcontracted out to an ever-expanding mass of specialists. A respiratory therapist…a speech pathologist…a gastrointestinal pediatric surgeon…a physical therapist…a thanatologist…

The thoughts he'd been holding back for the past three months flooded his consciousness. Where was Armageddon when you needed it? His whole miserable species had stuck around for 200,000-odd years. It had gotten on long enough to crown its rich heritage with one final achievement: making itself wholly obsolete. With little left to do but replicate and die, it was nearing the day when, having used up the earth, it could only do the latter. Quailing as he envisioned the end, he instinctively reached out for a guardrail. But he grasped only air.

Even as he stumbled sideways, reflexively flailing his arms, Corbett kept his sense of humor. The installation crew hadn't taped off the ledge. Now he was falling away from it at mounting speed. Talk about an expensive oversight! This was going to cost UTech millions in sales. He howled at the hilarity of it all. As he hurtled toward the bottom of the spotless abyss, he remembered another meaning for the word "ave." It meant farewell. Ω

Serving Time

Written By
David Reinersmann

"What is the nature of reality, and what is our place in it? What is consciousness, and does it affect the world it observes?

"Welcome to BBC Radio's *Our World*, today, as we tackle what are perhaps the most fundamental questions that have ever faced humanity. I'm William Haverford. Thank you for listening. I offer further thanks and welcome to the great many additional listeners here in the U.K. and abroad that I'm sure are tuning in this evening, most of whom for the first time.

"Now, my guest tonight needs little introduction, but it is my habit and, to be perfectly frank, my prerogative. So I shall crack on. I'm joined today by Dr. Dame Eloise Chattopadhyay, DBE, a research fellow at the University of Mumbai, a teaching professor of quantum matter at the Cavendish Laboratory here at the University of Cambridge, and a Dame Commander of the Most Excellent Order of the British Empire."

Haverford struggles, pausing. He continues after a moment, his warm, aristocratic voice uncertain. "I'm not quite sure how to address you, Dr. Dame Chattopadhyay–"

A smile apparent in her tone, she replies, "Please, please, just call me Eloise. That's all such a mouthful."

Laughing lightly, relieved, he says, "We are certainly in agreement there, thank you. And please call me Will. Now, *Eloise*, tell us a little bit about *you* before we get to the, um, revelations you have for us. We're going to ease into our subject today. You are of Indian descent, but with a name such as Eloise, I assume you were born here?"

"I wasn't, actually, but my parents had known they were going to move to the U.K. for some time before I was born and, as is the habit of some immigrants, gave me an English name to help me fit in a bit more easily."

"And how do you feel about that decision? Did it help?"

"Well, I suppose I have to give that most frustrating of answers: yes and no." She laughs lightly. "We moved to Glasgow when I was only a few months old, giving me this decidedly non-Indian accent."

Haverford interjects: "And a lovely one it is."

Chattopadhyay continues: "Thank you very much. My English given name and decidedly not English surname have raised some eyebrows over the years. It's perhaps been a bit easier to have only half of my name be unpronounceable. Though I must say that you did quite well with it."

"I've had a lot of practice here on this program. Now, you're a fellow at the University of Mumbai—is that where your family is from originally?"

"Oh no, we're from Khorda, in Orissa, quite a long ways from Mumbai. I was offered a position there somewhat recently in more of an honorary sense, given my success at Cambridge."

Haverford clears his throat. "Explain to our listeners how you got your DBE, if you would."

Chattopadhyay responds, clearly embarrassed by the scrutiny, "Oh, certainly. It was awarded for work that led me here, actually—to these revelations, as you called them. It really was quite a telephone call, I must say. And there really is a ceremony with a sword and everything! Very much like a fairy tale, except the men were all in suits of cloth rather than armor. That was a bit disappointing, I must say."

Haverford and Chattopadhyay share a laugh before he continues. "Now, perhaps that we've gotten a bit more comfortable, we can begin to move into your recent scientific discoveries. Are you feeling all right to move on?"

She takes a deep breath. "Yes, all ready. I must say, I'm not quite sure how to handle interviews just yet. It's such a foreign world to me."

He replies, understanding. "You'll do just fine. Just ignore the microphones and such, and think about having a conversation with me. We're just two people having an ordinary conversation about humanity's role in the Universe that's being broadcast to millions of listeners. Nothing could be more normal."

Allowing time for her short laugh, the interviewer continues. "We're going to go through this piece by piece. You've told parts of your story in a few other venues, but here we are going to be *thorough*—no stone unturned, as they say. We'll start at the beginning: You've built a time machine."

*　*　*

A great, shining monstrosity, her machine took up a good deal of the gymnasium-sized laboratory. Chattopadhyay looked upon her creation with a curious mix of pride and trepidation. This collection of tubes, wiring, steel plating, lights, switches, enormous canisters, and miniature transistors represented years of research and thousands of labor hours. And she was about to use two of its few easily identifiable components: the chair and the big red button.

*　　*　　*

The interviewer interrupts her description. "There really is a big red button on it?"

"I couldn't resist," replies the inventor with a smile.

*　　*　　*

The Machine, as the research group had taken to calling it, had components that broke ground in several disciplines. The nuclear reactor was the most powerful of its kind relative to its size; the shielding surrounding it was of a material lighter and more effective than any used before; the force field that would surround the entire Machine was a technology heretofore entirely unrealized; even the chair was from an experimental aircraft designed by the Americans. Chattopadhyay climbed into the seat formerly occupied by a soldier intent on killing others and recalled the old axiom of beating swords into plowshares.

As she ran through her checklists for the last time, she fervently and earnestly hoped that her creation would bring further knowledge, peace, and understanding to the world.

Failing that, Eloise quipped to herself, *we could actually beat a few dozen plowshares out of it.*

The moment had come at long last. Having received well-wishes from the rest of the principle team, given the last of the warnings to onlookers, instructions to research assistants, and prayers to every god she could name, Chattopadhyay pressed the big red button, flying backward in time.

*　　*　　*

"Please, explain to us what you saw as you traveled backward in time."

As Eloise starts to answer, Haverford interrupts. "No, sorry. Sorry. First, I want to offer you a heartfelt congratulations on achieving even that much. On achieving something that we have wondered about, written about, and fervently wished for since the idea was first posited by Samuel Madden in 1773. You, Dr. Dame Eloise Chattopadhyay, DBE, have traveled in time. I wish to thank you and congratulate you on behalf of all people everywhere."

Taken aback by this sudden effusiveness, Chattopadhyay replies. "Thank—thank you, Mr. Haverford. That was really quite kind of you to say." She pauses. "Samuel Madden?"

He laughs. "That's one of those facts—those nuggets—that I was so hoping to use today. He was arguably the first writer to propose the idea of traveling *backward* in time. An angel brings descriptions of the far future back to him—from 1999, actually. The idea of traveling *forward* in time is much older indeed—a story from Hindu mythology perhaps as old as twenty-eight hundred years. Now, sorry, please do go on. What did you see as you traveled through time?"

"I'll tell you what I expected to see. I expected to see events literally flowing backward. We often express time in that way, *flowing* like a river, and so I expected that I would see that river flow backward around me. Unfortunately, at the great speeds which I was traveling through time, everything was just a sort of beige color. There were shadows and bits of movement within the beige, but they were either tiny and fast or enormous and incredibly slow."

Haverford questions, "At what rate were you traveling at this point, just after you took off, so to speak?"

Chattopadhyay speaks with the confidence of a scientist discussing her work, having lost her prior nervousness. "The initial rate at which I traveled was about one year of objective time for every thirty seconds of Machine time. I traveled at that rate for twenty-three minutes—which, incidentally, is the precise amount of time it takes for a person to get sick of the color beige."

The volume of Haverford's voice increases on radio sets all over the world as he leans in to the microphone, her quip barely registering as his fascination takes over. "And you stopped there, forty-six years ago, in, let's see, 1966?"

Feeling the tenor of the conversation change somewhat, Chattopadhyay replies quickly and succinctly. "No, at that point I slowed down my travel so that I could make out a bit of the 'river' flowing past. My reduced rate was now roughly one year of objective time for every five minutes of Machine time. I stayed at this speed for several hours, observing with fascination Cambridge University's changes throughout the years."

*   *   *

The modern laboratory gave way to an older building, in which the Machine would have taken up several of the small rooms common in the fifties and sixties. Situated just off a small street, the building was of light-colored bricks and small, white-trimmed windows, looking more like a residential building than a physics laboratory. The sky was a strange sort of deep blue color, coated with the white haze of spinning stars as day and night blurred together. There were no people or animals to be seen outside, though there was an indistinct blurring on the roadway that seemed to be the path of traveling vehicles. Chattopadhyay experimented by slowing down her progress through time until she could just make out cars zipping by, running backward at unbelievable speeds. After her curiosity was sated, she returned the scene to its original beige swirl.

*   *   *

"That's an absolutely stunning scene you've painted in my mind and the minds of all our listeners, I'm sure. Now, there's something I'm curious about. One problem of *theorized* time travel doesn't seem to have affected your Machine. That is, that as the Earth revolves around the Sun in space, why wouldn't your time machine have stayed behind? Why did it stay tied to the Earth and not rematerialize you in the black of space? Before you answer, I must say that I'm quite glad it didn't, for your sake."

Chattopadhyay replies, "Actually, that was one of the reasons for the force field around the Machine—it would have protected me from the vacuum and unfiltered radiation of outer space. But to your main question, there's a fault in the premise, apparently. Everything, as Einstein proved, is relative.

"And I should add, as an aside, despite the fact that Albert Einstein was wrong on time travel does not mean he was wrong on other things, nor does it take away from the enormity of his achievements. Some newspapers have picked up this 'Cambridge woman destroys Einstein's theories' rubbish, and it's unfair and simply incorrect.

"So everything is relative. Motion is impossible to measure without a reference point. With respect to the roadway, a police officer might measure your speed at one hundred twenty kilometers per hour, *tsk tsk*. But taking reference from you or your passenger, your car is perfectly still. But don't try that at traffic court.

"So the Earth spins about its axis at a rate of about half a kilometer per second—that is to say, that's the *speed* of the Earth's crust taking the center of the Earth as a reference point. With respect to the Sun, the Earth is revolving around at a rate of about thirty kilometers per second. With respect to the center of the Milky Way, the Earth is moving between two hundred twenty and two hundred eighty kilometers per second, depending on its position around the Sun."

Haverford asks, deeply curious, "How did you know that the Machine would take the specific bit of ground it was on as a reference point?"

Chattopadhyay lets out a deep breath. "We didn't. That's what the force field was for, in part. And as it turned out, to get to one of our main points today, we needed it."

*   *   *

As the minutes ticked by in the Machine, Chattopadhyay approached the turn of the 20th century. The beige continued uninterrupted, and she busied herself maintaining instruments and planning the next stop. Roughly two minutes after that, everything changed. When the calendar measuring objective time ran past August 26, 1896, Eloise screamed.

She was in the blackness of space, alone, protected only by her force field. *It's so black*, she thought, and then said aloud, "*Black?* Where are all the stars?"

Chattopadhyay quickly slowed the Machine's temporal progress and stared in wonder and confusion as the blackness gave way to a confusing light show.

The stars and galaxies were winking in and out in thin, long arcs, like diamonds shining as a beam of light passes over them. She twisted and turned in her seat, seeing the same surreal scene play out all around her. This wasn't star creation and destruction—the same stars were turning on and off. *Impossible*, she thought.

*   *   *

"When did you figure out what was happening?" asks a disturbed Haverford.

After another deep breath out, Chattopadhyay responds. "Not until I got back home. Which was another unexplained phenomenon. I didn't need to tell the Machine to stop on the date that I left. It took me back to the very second from which I'd departed. For a moment, I feared that no one would believe that I'd traveled, but the look on my face must have said it all.

"My face must have said too much, actually, because the mood in the lab was quite subdued. There was no cheering or celebrating, just hurried work to be done and hours of video and sensor readings to pour over. At first, I thought I would pass out from the exhaustion, but my confusion kept me awake. There were several conclusions we came to, and I'll run through them one by one. No stone unturned, right?"

Haverford is uncharacteristically silent.

"First, to explain why the Machine reappeared when it did. The future hasn't happened yet, so of course I can't go there. Traveling into the future at a rate greater than one second per second without differences in speed among moving and stationary observers, is, we can assert with some degree of confidence, impossible.

Haverford questions, "Well, it's possible that your Machine just isn't capable of it, isn't it? That for some reason it can't go past its originating point in time?"

"Yes, that's why I qualified my statement somewhat with those wiggle words 'some degree of confidence.' In all our hours of study, we still haven't been able to come up with anything approaching an explanation. We're left with the theory that since the Machine was able to travel forward in time, but only up to the moment it left, there was simply no future to go to. We absolutely concede that there may be an alternative explanation that we're not seeing."

After taking a deep breath, Haverford pushes on. "Right. What are these other conclusions then?"

"Our second conclusion comes to us, in a way, from a woman named Besse Berry Cooper, née Brown. She's a lovely American lady living in Monroe, Georgia. Aside from her wonderful personality and disposition, there are two things of great note about Besse. She is one hundred and sixteen years old, making her the oldest living human being at the moment, and her birthday is August 26, 1896."

Chattopadhyay lets that fact sit on the table a moment, waiting for Haverford to respond. When he finally does, he speaks with a nervous tilt to his voice. "I suppose you're going to tell our listeners that this is not a coincidence."

"It is not in the least a coincidence. This fact leads us to our second revelation about the nature of the Universe and to the first about our place in it. Reality only exists as long as there is a sentient being alive to observe it, or—and this is the tricky bit—*to have observed it.*

"In a sense, only can things in a potential living memory exist. Once I crossed the border, so to speak, into a time which no currently living person was alive to have observed, the things which could have been observed ceased to exist. Before the moment when Besse Berry Cooper was born, nothing exists."

A thoughtful Haverford responds. "Now, hang on a minute. I mean, the day-old Mrs. Cooper—or then, of course, Miss Brown—couldn't have observed the Sun, the entire Earth, and all the rest of the planets and such. There has to be something larger at work here."

"That was precisely our first thought as well. But it appears that consciousness is a unique force in the Universe. And I want to head off the debate over the beginning of life straight away." Chattopadhyay speaks now as if from a prepared text. "I do not propose to definitively set the beginning of meaningful life at birth. I am only saying that fundamental forces at work in the Universe 'recognize' an independent observer at the moment that it is physically separated from its parent. When life truly begins is not at question, nor is it a question for which I choose to give an answer or opinion."

"You've practiced that a time or two, haven't you?" Haverford asks, a smile in his tone.

Again, Chattopadhyay laughs quietly. "Neither philosophy nor politics are in my bailiwick, although I've tread awfully close this past year."

The interviewer returns to the subject. "So how is it that Miss Brown is responsible, so to speak, for the existence of things which she has never laid eyes on?"

"This is a crucial point. Miss Brown, and later Mrs. Cooper, was a school teacher. She did not have the great wealth necessary to see even every continent on Earth, much less scour the entire night sky to observe all that we have evidence of and all that existed when I went back to the day of her birth. That's absolutely right. We have two hypotheses on this.

"The first is that all those things exist which she not only *did* observe but all those things which it was *possible* for her to have observed. This of course means that when you close the door to your bedroom, all of your things do not disappear, and when no one happens to be looking at Betelgeuse, it still very much exists. This is, however, highly subjective, and the Universe is anything but subjective.

"The other, which resonates somewhat more with me, is that at the time of her birth, her consciousness began to exist outside that of another's—that is, her mother's. Once that moment occurred, everything within a certain as-yet-undetermined range of that consciousness came into existence. Or rather, was further verified by that consciousness, as there were nearly two billion humans alive at that time."

Clearing his throat, Haverford asks, "You say the second theory 'resonates' with you. Is that as accurate as we can get on this?"

Chattopadhyay sighs. "Unfortunately, yes. We really have no way to experiment with this. As you probably noted, *I* was an observer before her birth, and the Sun, Earth, and so on did not reappear because I was there to observe them. Either being a time traveler means that I don't have a continuity with the pre-observation past, or the force field around the Machine somehow protected the Universe from my consciousness. I am quite inclined to believe the former.

"For me, the second question this raises is on the definition of consciousness. Are dogs and cats conscious? Dolphins and other intelligent animals? We can't be certain, unfortunately; we can only say that certain animals certainly do not have the consciousness required to observe the Universe. Bowhead whales have been known to live over two hundred years, several species of tortoise live well over one hundred fifty, and some coral are thousands of years old. These animals apparently do not possess the minimum capacity to keep the Universe in existence. Until we see a two-hundred-year-old dog or dolphin or what have you, we won't be able to answer that question any more precisely."

Haverford's curiosity is evident in his voice as he asks, "So what effect does consciousness have on the Universe? On matter and energy?"

"Well, the primary effect, as small a term as that is for its impact, is to call the Universe into being. The combined observation of sentient beings gives the Universe a continuity that I'm not sure it would otherwise have. However, the Universe still follows fundamental laws: gravity, relativity, Newton's laws of motion, etc. We also want to be careful to avoid claiming that humankind has created the Universe. In fact—" Chattopadhyay pauses, not sure if she should continue with this line of conversation just yet. She takes a deep breath, lets it out. "In fact, we have proof that we are not. We are not the only ones doing the observing."

There is a pause, a nervous silence. "I beg your pardon?"

Chattopadhyay settles in, ready to lecture. "If you recall, I said that I could see other stars, blinking in and out in great sweeping arcs. These are, of course, other sentient races observing the cosmos. The sweepings, really only visible during movement through time, are artifacts of their telescopes and other machinery extending their consciousness's powers of observation. Given the degree of arc of the many points of origin we observed, these societies have powers of observation well beyond our own.

"Upon reviewing the recordings of the journey, we determined that there are no less than 350 other observing civilizations within the observational powers of the equipment on the Machine. Humanity is not alone in the Universe."

Haverford stumbles. "Eloise, you have again made a discovery that in any other conversation would absolutely floor me. I feel as though you will next tell me you discovered the human soul. God, maybe you have." He pauses, grasping for a handhold on the situation. "Wait a moment, you mentioned Newton a moment ago—that brings to mind something else. What about the law of conservation of mass and energy? Isn't what being wildly violated here?"

Chattopadhyay is clearly excited by this question. "Yes! We thought so too at first. The amount of matter being destroyed is staggering. The Sun by itself weighs on the order of two times ten-to-the-thirty kilograms. That's a two with thirty naughts behind it. Where does all this matter go?

"But then I thought of the stars winking out. Surely that can't be—I'd never be able to see the arc of the observation passing over a star. The light from those stars would hit my eye at various times, as they are all at different distances from my position. And that led us to our answer. The matter isn't being destroyed and created; the Universe itself is. Matter and energy—the concepts themselves, not just the actual matter and energy are being affected. Even the light traveling out from a given star ceases to exist when that star is not being observed. It's not that the Sun, Earth, Moon, asteroids, and comets of August 1896 will wink out of existence when Mrs. Cooper passes on. *That part of the Universe will no longer exist!*"

"Then your force field wasn't protecting you from the vacuum of space, but from…what, nothingness, non-existence?"

"The vacuum of space is nothing like what most people think of—it's actually quite full of elementary particles constantly moving about. I have no idea what exposure to the nothingness of POP time would do to a person."

"POP time?"

22

Chattopadhyay snorts a short laugh. "Ah, right. Pre-Observation Period. The time before the oldest currently living observer's birth."

Haverford lets out a deep breath. "I'm a bit afraid to ask, Eloise. Do you have any other revelations for us? What else did your research turn up?"

She laughs a relieved laugh, "No, no, that's quite enough for me, thanks."

Haverford's tone shifts dramatically, now gentle and probing. "Then I'd like to ask you about why we're having this interview where we are. Tell us, in your own words this time, without the barristers, judges, and reporters. Tell us why you're in prison."

Chattopadhyay's mood instantly changes. The thrill of reliving her story is gone, replaced by the dread of reliving the next one. Her facade of normality has cracked, giving way to the broken woman beneath. She slides her chair back from the table slightly, the steel legs grating on the concrete floor. Careful listeners can also hear the imposing guards in two corners of the room bristle slightly, ready for violence from even the most peaceful of prisoners.

"The town motto of Monroe, GA, where Mrs. Besse Berry Cooper is from, is 'Do right.' Did you know that, Will?"

"I didn't," he replies with a lilt, curious about where she's taking the conversation.

"I thought so long and so hard about what that meant, about what 'doing right' means. And I came to the awful conclusion that it meant to do the most good for the largest possible group of people—that classic Utilitarian argument rang true for me.

"Of course I regret what I did. Of course it was an evil thing. Of course the pain I've given those four families will never go away. And of course, I didn't kill myself."

She musters up the courage to go on, taking long, deep breaths. Will Haverford sits with her in silence for a moment, letting her gather herself.

"Will, I killed four people. Four brilliant, beautiful people, because it could have very well saved every other life on this planet, and perhaps every sentient life in the Universe. The ends, I truly hate to say, justify the means.

"There were really only five people who knew how the Machine worked— every nut, bolt, switch, and pedal. These five people worked together in a way that brought us as close as family, let our minds gel in a way I've never seen. We were a *unit*, Will, acting like a super-organism, like an ant colony. I firmly believe that I was part of something beautiful.

"The temptation, Will, was instantaneous. The one question that everyone asked was, 'Can you change the past?'"

Her voice begins to rise, more and more emphasis and emotion in each successive word. "Of course it was—what else do we think about when we imagine going to the past? Kill Hitler, Pol Polt, Stalin, Milošević. Save a loved one. Stop a war! *Can we do it?*"

Eloise pauses, lowering her voice back to a conversational level. "I'm proud to say that the answer to that question is 'I don't know.' I didn't try.

"I was the only one who wasn't tempted, who didn't think of it immediately after realizing that the Machine was really going to work. I was the only one who didn't have a cause to champion, who believed in the sanctity of the timeline."

Will's question is quiet. "Is that why you killed them, because they were going to change things in the past?"

"No, no, I said we were a team—a *unit*! We talked, discussed, debated fiercely. The unit was fighting, but the unit survived intact. We all decided that none of us must ever alter the timeline—that it was more important than anything, even the project. Even us.

"When I went back in time, I was tempted beyond imagination, beyond *reason*, to alter, to fix history. I realized the enormity of my power, and I decided to land the Machine in the far, far past and destroy it. But once I saw the blackness, I knew that wasn't possible. And once I realized the importance of our discoveries, I knew I had to return to the present to make them known. But I also realized that time travel had to be prevented at all costs.

"We destroyed the Machine after only a few uses. We sacked everyone else in the laboratory and took apart each individual piece ourselves, destroying any component that was at all unique and every bit of data related to the construction. But I knew there was more to do. We all had to die."

Here Eloise breaks up, unable to continue for a moment. When she resumes speaking, her voice is quiet and broken, cracking with her grief and guilt. "I got a gun, and I shot them. I shot all of them, because we all had to die. We could be made to talk, to give our secrets to the government, the Americans, the Russians—somebody would make us construct another one.

"I said I believe that we five were special, and it's true. We were the secret, at least for now, to time travel. It'll be a long time before anyone is ever able to do it again, and between now and then, we have to convince everyone that we were right about the timeline. That whoever goes back doesn't change anything. It could destroy *everything*. We don't know how fragile the Universe is, and there's no room for experimentation. It's more important than any of our lives."

Will says quietly, reluctantly, "Except yours?"

Eloise sobs. "I couldn't do it. It's so much…harder."

William Haverford draws into himself for a moment, quiet and contemplative, reemerging as the calm, composed, erudite host that the nation has known for three decades. When he speaks again, he is no longer unsure, quiet, or emotional. He speaks as if from a prepared text, though no script exists. His speech is occasionally punctuated by quiet sobs from the broken woman across the table, barely audible over his voice.

"We don't like our heroes to be complex in the real world. In film and television, we can root for a flawed anti-hero. But in life, we want our villains in black and our heroes—and heroines—in white. We rarely get what we want. The genius, heroic, *flawed* woman who sits in front of me will go on trial tomorrow, and she will certainly be convicted of her heinous crimes and sentenced to life in prison. This is a just and proper action.

"But just as our heroes are flawed, so are our own stories. Our past is not something to be improved upon. For just as no person is perfect, neither is any history perfect. To attempt to perfect a person would destroy him or her, just as any attempt to improve the past would likely leave it worse, if not absolutely unravel the fabric of the Universe.

"We, the human race, will soon again possess a power of unbelievable proportions. We have faced this test again and again as our mastery over our

Universe grows more and more complete. The day may come when tearing apart and rebuilding atoms is as simple as building a piece of furniture, when engineering a child is no more a bother than cooking dinner and traveling through time is as simple as driving to the grocer's. We must face these issues with far more humility than we have in the past. We must respect the powers with which we are meddling, or we will all surely perish in the attempt.

"Besides, there are at least a few hundred other races out there who we'll have to meet eventually. We don't want to be the ones who almost destroy the Universe, do we? It would be awfully embarrassing."

Haverford clears his throat. "This is William Haverford on *Our World*. My guest has been Dr. Dame Eloise Chattopadhyay: scholar, time traveler, murderer. And, at least in my view, hero. Goodnight." Ω

Old Faithless

Written By
L. L. Hill

"Hang on!"

The warning came as the Mars Surface Vehicle had already bounced high in thin gravity. A rear wheel flashed outside the porthole, in a slow motion spin yet seeming to try to overtake the two in front of it. Jean grabbed at a hand strap and missed as she bounced to the limit of her seat harness. Laughter filled the MSV communication system.

Jean Percotte, thirty-two years old, a qualified physician and CSA specialist now bound for the South Pole Water Station, cursed in silent vehemence in four languages. Her head had almost been punched back into her suit, and she braced herself between hand straps and seat harness to refit herself into suit and helmet. Trim from years of yoga, her brown eyebrows were straight under curly brown hair and over snapping brown eyes.

"Thanks for the early warning. Why the change of scenery?" she asked.

With a big, toothy smile on his face, the navigator, Slim, looked back at her. Without a helmet, his eyes were glacial blue shards. He and the driver, Chip, exchanged a swift nudge and a wink.

"The way to a man's heart is through his stomach, and we don't want to be late for breakfast." Each word hung in the air of the MSV like Earth's orbiting garbage.

Jean watched the wheels outside traverse the red regolith of a seldom used track as she thought and then spoke carefully. "How long have you been on station? Home and hamburgers must be a daily fantasy for you by now."

Slim licked back flecks of sprayed saliva. "No fantasy at all. Home is about twenty miles from here. It has hamburgers, pizza, French fries, and even a little moonshine from the still. One brew is called Phobos, one Deimos. We'd be happy to make dinner sometime—might loosen you up."

"I think that I'm about as loose as I'm going to get, but thanks for being concerned about me." Jean wondered if her contempt was visible through her visor. She was not tired, just annoyed. Flexing the tension out of her hands, she questioned why, from a population of ten billion, NASA had felt obliged to employ two jackasses on Mars.

"You know, if you want to get anything done around here, it pays to loosen up, a lot." Slim's smile displayed very pointed canines and the warmth of the last polar bear on Earth, a caged and pacing ball of rage.

"I've always chosen professional decorum over personal desires and have had issues with no one," Jean replied. Almost no one. A randy octopus of a professor and roommate locked out prodded her memory.

Mocking laughter filled the MSV, and she wondered if the black box were turned on. They did not seem to be a pair that relished witnesses. And they were provoking.

With the sun overhead, shadows were few and the terrain stark and forbidding. Red and black rocks were covered with a variable layer of white, spiky frost that gave the landscape a cream wash. Someone, somewhere should be watching and tracking the MSV on the Mars Positioning System. Hopefully, not all the Martian crew was as rude as this pair.

They were now driving down the radial arm of one of the geyser spider webs, a shallow depression about two yards wide at the bottom and three to four wide at the top. Carved by the temperature differential of carbon dioxide laden water to the carbon dioxide frost, the sides were traced with dry rivulets. Some ice coated puddles were opened by the MSV's wheels. Away in the distance, limp flags marked the route that they should have been following.

With black lichen and tufts of green and loden, the barren landscape would have been similar to training grounds in the Arctic and Antarctic. In the dark, it was much colder than the coldest spots on Earth. One rock, perhaps a volcanic piece, looked like chocolate ice cream cake. If she could, she'd check on it later.

"Seriously, if that is possible, why did we detour?" she asked.

"Well, the scenic route is two miles shorter but not necessarily rougher. The detour is to take us around the cyrogeyser Old Faithless. Of course, it's named for lack of reliability, unlike an earthly near namesake, Old Faithful, which blew up with the super volcano of 2133. With the sun shining, it will be blowing," Slim smiled and winked.

With puffy cheeks, he seemed very not slim, and Jean wondered if he had acquired his nickname as an abbreviation of 'slime'. Still, the pair of rule breakers might be persuaded to stop and observe the geyser with a false promise. She was aware of a geyser field between the landing area and the station that had been built on water ice at the planetary pole. There might be one of the irregular eruptions, and these had been little studied. Like the hydrant springs of the Arctic, meter high fountains on the tundra that had been described for two hundred years, the exact processes triggering the seasonal Martian geysers was still unknown, yet speculation about their cause and the potential for life in them had continued since their discovery.

"And we're detouring in proximity to a periodic geyser to save time or shorten life expectancy?" Jean's lips curled down.

"To save time, of course. We can stop, and get to know each other better, a lot better, and still be at base before the CO sends a search party," Chip said with a chilling purr as he watched her in a mirror.

"Oh, you have an interest in studying geyser activity," Jean said with an exaggerated sigh. "Are you both mildly claustrophobic? I ask as a physician." It could not hurt to remind them that she would participate in their psyche evaluations.

They looked at each other. "No ma'am, not at all. We're just relaxed and comfortable when surrounded by a hostile environment," Chip answered. They both snickered.

"Even one that you created? And your CO is comfortable with you violating his protocol to be fully suited in transit? Or is that 'our' little secret? Clearly he knows that we're off track." Steam fogged her visor. Yoga was not working while under duress.

"It's no secret, ma'am. CO knows what we do and why. Protocol up here is just like Earth—a paper tiger of rhetoric to flap when something goes wrong."

Chip steered gently to the easiest path for the MSV as he spoke. Jean admired his deft touch as she questioned his morals. Then she noticed a quiver of the digits. Could they be affected by oxygen or other gas toxicity, she wondered.

Slim added with a greasy, sideways grin, "And we do like to be ready to serve up a 'quickie' at the end of the trail. Your predecessor, Dr. Sugimi Chin, a well written and well read lady, had no objections to broadening her horizons, especially when told that she would have an 'accident' otherwise."

Jean's boot clipped Slim on the side of the head.

"Hey, only jok…"

Slim's sentence ended with his face smeared into the forward window. Next to him, also with no seat harness, Chip was bounced out of his seat and away from the control stick. Jean would later try to convince herself that she had deliberately kicked Slim, but in reality, Chip and Slim had lost track of their proximity to Old Faithless and had driven the MSV into a cold, carbon dioxide ice, water, basalt, and sulphur laden chemical spout that held them briefly cradled in an umbrella fan before crashing them onto the ice and bouncing them onto the rock below the gaping geyser orifice.

Flipped and somersaulted around on the short leash granted by the seat harness, Jean collapsed in a white space suit pile when the MSV finally came to rest. An all-encompassing, thundering roar that shook her to her core and rat-a-tat of rock and ice pellets slowly receded. She screamed in stress and frustration in the near dark below the ice.

Sitting up to a low level cacophony of snaps and crackles, Jean assessed her situation. She had no doubt that Slim and Chip had not survived. She moved slowly, checking herself over and feeling for sharp pieces of wreckage. Very carefully, she turned on helmet and wrist lights. A camera switched on with the helmet light. She saw that her pack had blown out of a window past the wrecks that had been Chip and Slim into the core of the geyser.

Jean checked both pearl mottled faces with an old fashioned mirror and an acoustic stethoscope from the MSV med pack. She opted to use Zulu time to record the time of death on her wrist touch pad.

That process completed, Jean crawled over them and stepped carefully to her pack through the fan of debris. It seemed to be the safest spot to sit, and she did. Regulations required that a black box record all MSV activities and MPS track all positions. The deceased were exhibits A and B that protocol had not been maintained.

That meant that help should not be expected quickly. This brought her to the question of where she should wait for help. Normal procedure was to wait with the 'downed craft,' but this 'downed craft' was in the mouth of a cyrogeyser that periodically shot out chemical soup at 160kph. One ride in the spout was enough.

Jean watched a tail of chunky grey soup drain over mottled black and red bedrock into the near meter-wide dark bore of the geyser. Undercut by the irregular blasting of the cyrogeyser, the striated ice lip was pocked with black basalt. The diameter of the melt bore hole in the ice was about fifteen meters, and the wreck of the MSV at about five by two meters in size sprawled between the rock and ice.

Climbing out was the required option and was theoretically easily accomplished with the cyrogeyser bore partially blocked by the MSV. There were, however, sharp bits sticking out, and any slip would result in a suit puncture. Less gravity also meant less physical control on an awkward climb. The dark, ominous gap between the ice and bedrock was nearly a meter in height. In the viscous space, particles brightened and dimmed in a pattern like breathing. Then there was a suck and a pause.

Inhaling quickly, Jean scrabbled back towards the MSV in search of an ice axe. Like a frightened animal, the geyser's respiration deepened to shakes and shudders as she wormed back over Chip and Slim to make it back to the partial safety of her seat harness. A chemical sand blasting soup hummed upwards, bouncing the MSV around. Her suit was spattered with white and black particulate as the eruption died away.

Panting, she disengaged the seat harness and opened a tool panel. She pulled out a shovel and an ice axe before closing the panel. No point in leaving too many blunt objects to fly around. The MSV had shifted, and the front window was now almost wedged under the ice. The next blast would likely be fatal to anyone inside.

Chip's remains had been flung out and hurled away. Slim's body now blocked half of the window, pinned grotesquely upside down. Jean slithered out and paused under the ice, chest heaving. The yard thick ice was almost clear, and she could see the basaltic ejaculate on the surface. Scored ripples like the palate of a mouth on the underside of the ice were painted a pale pink. At first, Jean thought that it was blood from Chip or Slim, but when their hearts stopped with asphyxiation, so did their circulation.

She caught her breath in delight. Her visor clunked on the ice. The pink was an intricate lace filigree in the ice. It was colored like watermelon snow, *Chlamydomonas nivalis* that thrived on the ice of glaciers, but possibly not requiring sunlight to survive. During a high school summer break in the Rocky Mountains,

Jean had explored the fringes of glaciers and peaks still distant from the pressing spires of civilization. They and other chemosynthetic plants had inspired her interest in outer space. Who knew what diseases could be cured by space bacteria?

Jean spiraled back into the MSV past Slim to grab sample bottles from a drawer. She left the drawer open as she scooted out. The point of the ice axe scraped pink shavings into a wide-mouthed jar. Taking a fleet moment to look in the jar, a patch of pink algae had melted out of the ice and formed a strand. She closed the jar on her delight and worked in desperate haste to fill another, feeling and listening for the warning breathes of an eruption.

With the lull and sighs of warning beginning, she crabbed out from under the ice and tossed her trophies up to the most level spot that she could see. Hammering shards flat, she stepped up onto the MSV, wedged the shovel in a crack as a brace, hammered the pick end in as far ahead as she could, and crawled up the ice. In a frenzy on top, she grabbed the samples and ran away from the maw of Old Faithless.

With wide leaps, she made good time and could see a flag ahead before the first effluent cascade began to fall. Jean slid to the ice and curled into a ball while salt and pepper rained on her. Like a popcorn machine that had popped all the corn, it slowed down and fizzled to a stop.

Jean got up slowly, every muscle shaking. Ahead, waiting outside an MSV, were two space suit clad specialists. Cradling the specimen bottles in one elbow and using the ice axe as a cane, she walked slowly over to them.

"I'm sorry. Slim and Chip are dead," she said, struggling to speak with control.

"No helmet and off road?" one faceless visor asked.

"Yes," she croaked.

"They were warned, in writing. Glad you made it. We'll get you to base and rested. For what it's worth, 'Sorry.' They had Dr. Chin in tears for less."

A gloved hand gently took the ice axe away. Jean looked at the prize scraped from the monster's palate and wondered what DNA would show. Ω

Enjoying our third issue?

A Clone Writes

Written By
John Grey

I read the newspapers.
I'm current. On page seven,
there's a time-line from test tube
to living and breathing,
and then a brief philosophical
contretemps between two professors
as to what it is exactly that lives and breathes
and sits in kitchen chairs, seeing himself in linotype,
in letterpress, while consuming
mouthfuls of milk and cereal.

I'm on TV. Sometimes the lead story.
Other times, at the end, a fluff piece
on whether or not I have a girlfriend.
Occasionally, covering high school sports,
they call me the kid with the bionic arm
though to be honest, my fast ball is just average

I'm used by this to the flash of cameras, to microphones
shoved in my face, to reporters asking such stupid questions as,
"How does it feel to be the offspring of a bio-lab?"
Truly, I don't remember what it was like
to be a dab of DNA, of chromosomes,
floating in the soup of life,
like I'm sure you don't remember pogoing in the womb.
And I don't feel any less human than you. Maybe more human
because I don't go around bothering people
at all hours of the day and night
to remind them that they're patented, not parented.

And to that religious mob outside my door
wailing "Child of Satan!"
I say, "Be thankful I'm not the bomb."
To the smarmy guy who badgers me with,
"Will you have kids the old fashioned way
or concoct them in the cellar?"
I come back, with "The vacuum cleaner and I
aren't thinking of starting a family just yet."

Aside from no boring family reunions
or tension-filled Sunday dinners with the folks,
or sibling jealousies and quarrels, parental arguments,
I'm as normal as can be.
Did I say aside from? I meant because of.

The Age of Discovery

Written By
Marc S. Cohen

From the moment she first set foot on campus, it was obvious to everyone there was something special about that Lexxeigh Mylar girl. And not just because she bears the name, brains, courage and contours of one of those old Action Comics superheroines (even her hair sports a tint of Superman Blue). Something about her makes a room go infrared as soon as she enters, turns spectrographs kaleidoscopic, and can send your head spinning like a marble round the perimeter of a parabolic radio dish. Just ask Kenny Pettiford. Just ask Benny Chan. Just ask Ram Ramachandran. They'll tell you that while she speaks the language of complex equations, can outsmart a Turing machine and solve the Sunday Times crossword in a couple nanoseconds, in every other way, the girl's pure magic.

And yet she's pure enigma, too. A paradox decked in denim. She will transfix you with those cerulean eyes of hers and make you feel like you are the only soul in the room, the only person whose research in the emerging field of computational exo-meteorology really matters, and the next minute she'll be glancing at her iPhone for trending tweets from #interstellar. Her favorite modifier is amazing, which she deploys in an almost indiscriminate and overused sort of way, whether to describe a breakthrough in String Theory or the Gala apple she just bit into. She can make you feel excited and sad and deliriously confused all at the same time; when you are in her company, you couldn't be more thrilled to be alive, and yet as soon as you part ways, it's all you can do not to hurl yourself out the nearest window. A big city girl with small-town ways, she is both real and unreal, a dream that passes in and out of materiality like some elemental fermion who could care less whether you classify it as a particle or a wave.

She was not yet twenty-seven when she arrived at the Institute, quite literally with moons in her eyes. She'd already earned a PhD in molecular biology three years before, having successfully mapped and regenerated, atom by atom, the molecular structure of a single stalk of celery (she is a strict vegan). The Trekkie dream of limitless food replication and the anti-poverty advocate's dream of an end to world hunger were now steps closer to fruition; yet when a member of her thesis defense panel facetiously asked if she was going to invent the holodeck next, she blinked her eyes as though uncomprehending and announced that she intended to pursue a second doctorate, this time in Astrophysics. Her quest entailed the discovery of exomoons.

That's right—not exoplanets, but exo*moons*. Extra solar planets were still all the rage in astronomy—there had already been some 150,000 catalogued by this time, and counting—but no one had yet figured a way to detect the lunar companions assumed to be orbiting them. The problem was simply that the little buggers were just too small for contemporary observational methods to catch them. So Lexxeigh devised a different approach. She was going to try searching for radio wave emissions instead. Scientists had recently started noticing the wave patterns produced by the interaction between some of the larger solar planets' magnetic fields and the ionospheres of their satellites. Those emitted by Jupiter's Io and Saturn's Titan were well documented. After refining the techniques used to study these moons, she set her sights on the dwarves roaming the Kuiper belt: that is, those frigid trans-Neptunian plutoid bodies hovering along the fringe of the solar system. By the time her classes ended, she already found a baby brother for Quaoar's Weywot and two little sisters for Orcus's Vanth. Sedna, meanwhile, was discovered to be the proud parent of twins.

Now she intended to target one of the nearest exoplanetary systems to Earth: 61 Virginis. The system sits just under 28 light years away. At its center is a G-type yellow dwarf slightly smaller than our sun. Originally three planets were known to circle the star, with sizes ranging from 5 to 25 times that of Earth, and with orbits that could fit snugly within Venus'. A fourth planet, 61 Virginis-e, was discovered later on, with a mass of only two or three Earths. With these facts at her fingertips, Lexxeigh booked time at the array at Hat Creek in northern California, and while still under the influence of that morning's acai berry, coconut milk, strawberry, and banana Amazon Warrior power shake, aimed her instruments at the heart of Virgo.

"Ingenious," said Kenny Pettiford.

"Brilliant," grinned Benny Chan.

"God, I could just eat her up," purred Ram Ramachandran.

That was seven months ago. About five months later, on a chilly October evening, with the nearby space heater crackling and Pink Floyd streaming from someone's Bluetooth speaker, she casually approached Kenny, who was busy calibrating the distance between his right hand and the two Milky Way bars hiding in his top desk drawer. At first, Kenny looked slightly nonplussed. It wasn't like Lexxeigh to sneak up on him like that. She usually kept to herself, immured inside her Spartan cubicle and mulling over her calculations like some

Carthusian staring down an ancient illuminated manuscript. She was about as elusive as a comet, to be sure, and just as non-committal, regularly declining invitations to join the others for after-hour drinks or a late-night foray into San Fran and a midnight munch-down in Chinatown. Maybe there was a future Mr. Lexxeigh out there, someone who might someday occupy the center of her own orbit, be the thermonuclear core to her corona, as it were, and with one potent flare send her whizzing off into the night like some light-speed breaching neutrino. Maybe Kenny had daydreamed about being that guy sometimes. But right now he wasn't daydreaming. The look on her face made this abundantly clear.

She needed a second opinion about something, and since there wasn't anyone more qualified around, she turned to Kenny. She showed him the paper she was holding, and his eyes creased.

He asked her what he was looking at. She told him. For months she had been plotting the wave transmissions they were picking up from the Virgo system. She had assumed them to be signs of lunar activity around the system's fourth planet, the one closest in size to Earth. But then she noticed something weird. The data looked different from that provided by Jupiter and Saturn, or even Quaoar. The wave patterns were irregular, too brief and sporadic to arise from lunar-planetary magnetic friction. But then, on closer inspection, you could discern an underlying order to it. They seemed to follow the trajectory of an obscure algorithm. Like a code.

Kenny was looking up at her directly now, mouth agape. True, she was photogenic enough to make a pulsar stop and pay attention, but that wasn't the reason for his sudden stupefaction.

Dark Side's "Eclipse" was streaming behind him.

"Are you saying what I think you're saying?"

Lexxeigh nodded. "The patterns aren't natural," she said. "They're from an artificial source. Someone is communicating out there."

*   *   *

He is a farmer with no imagination, and so he doesn't usually dream. If you were to ask him what he dreams, he will tell you he dreams of nothing. He dreams he is dreaming. He dreams he is dreaming about dreaming. And when he wakes up, he remembers nothing except dreaming about dreaming. But only for a moment. A moment after he awakens, all his dreams dissolve like antacid in a glass of water.

Today, he wakes up on the sofa with a stiff neck. The TV is on. He fell asleep before turning it off, like he does most nights. Not that he actually watches; more like the screen is just something to rest his stare on, a place to direct a pair of eyes weary of looking, eyes that lost interest in looking long ago, that now just look because they have to, the way a literate person reads because he has to, because you cannot *not* look at a word and fail to read it, even if you don't understand what it is you're reading. Likewise, you don't have to understand what the heads talking on the screen are saying, though you look at and listen to them anyway. Until you finally get up to shut the damn thing off and head for the kitchen to make yourself some breakfast.

He lives alone but still manages to keep busy. Today, he will work on his old tractor, which he has been venturing to restore for going on a year now. Then he will head into the woods to chop firewood. They are predicting a long winter, and though he has enough fuel to last him for three, he likes to be especially prepared. Later that afternoon, the man is supposed to come to look at the well. The water pressure is low; he hasn't bathed all week.

After eating a couple sausages with toast and a small plate of scrambled eggs, he walks out to the shed. On his way, he passes the garden. Several tomato vines have been pulled down. It's the 'coons again. He walks into the dim light inside the shed, and waits for his vision to adjust. The tractor is in disarray. The engine and steering wheel are missing. Other parts are scattered all over the floor.

Figures. He's grown accustomed to things falling apart and disappearing. First his marriage fell apart, and after his wife left, the living room furniture disappeared one piece at a time, until only the sofa and the television remained. The same thing happened in the kitchen. All she left him with were a few dishes, a pot, and a frying pan. His daughter moved all her things out, too. He might have half expected them to take him, too, but they stopped short of doing so.

He exhales, gathers the tractor parts together, and deposits them in a crate, then reaches for his axe.

The woods are just beyond the perimeter of the southern field. He cuts down three saplings that morning, until the pain in his neck becomes too bothersome to continue. Setting down his axe, he walks to the edge of the woods and rests on a log for a spell. When he returns, the axe is gone. Figures. He searches all over, but finds nothing. Then he returns to gather the wood he chopped, and he sees the axe sticking out of the stump. Right where he left it.

"Maybe my luck is changing," he mutters.

When he leaves the woods, he spots a raccoon carcass stretched out alongside the trail. Its throat is deeply gashed.

Back at the house, a man is standing on his front porch. His pallor resembles drywall, but his eyes burn like cinder. His hands tremble slightly. It's hard to say if the farmer notices. It's just as likely he's too consumed with the heartburn that's been vexing him since breakfast to wonder if the man is suffering a similar affliction.

"You must be here to look at the well," he says. "Come. I'll bring you 'round the side to take a look."

When they reach it, there is no trace of the wellhead. It was there yesterday, but now it's gone. The earth must have swallowed it.

"Wait a minute, guy," he says. "I got an idea."

He leaves the man a moment and goes to the barn. Up on a high shelf is a branch from an old apple tree shaped like a Y.

"It's how I find water for the tiling," he says after returning.

The man does not answer. The trembling in his hands has grown worse.

The farmer walks toward the stoop, holding the branch out so that the stem points straight ahead. He paces approximately seven steps from the house. The branch does not move. He paces another seven steps, and the branch begins to sag. After a few more attempts, he declares the precise spot where the well should be. He digs down a little with the tip of his boot, and uncovers the end of a pipe.

The man still hasn't said a word. His hands are now shaking so much that his arms have begun to flail.

"Say, are you okay, fella?" asks the farmer.

The man does not respond. He just stares at the farmer and gestures like a rabid animal. He tilts his head back and begins jumping around the lawn.

The farmer shrugs, then asks him, "Ain't you gonna' check the well now?"

The man does not respond. He hops back to the top of the drive and takes off down the road. He doesn't appear to care one iota about the water pressure.

That night, the farmer hears a loud crash outside. It sounds like it's come from the field next door. He puts on his boots and coat and hurries out the back door. At first, he encounters nothing unusual. The ground is coated in mist, and the only light for miles emanates from the house or his flashlight. He approaches the field and looks hard into the night. He calls out once or twice, but there is no reply.

He circles the perimeter of the house, then spots a pair of tire tracks cutting across his front yard. He follows the tracks into the adjacent field, as far as fifty paces from the edge of the lawn. Then the tracks disappear.

The farmer scratches his head. They certainly look like ordinary tire tracks. Maybe the mist is playing tricks with his eyesight. He looks around to see if the tracks resume a little further ahead. They do not. He walks further into the field. His boots are caked in mud, each step sinking deeper into the soft earth. There is no sign of the tire tracks. What's more, there is no sign of the crash that first woke him. From the sound of it, he might have expected to find a vehicle or two blasted into spare parts. Instead, he encounters only mud.

He walks back and surveys the road in front of his house. There is no sign of an accident. The tracks lead off the side of the road, but there is no point of re-entry, no skid marks on the pavement. No metal fragments anywhere. It's as if the field has swallowed the vehicle whole.

He goes back and looks into the shed. He opens the door and aims his flashlight inside. The tractor is still there, still missing its steering wheel and engine. The box of parts remains on the bench where he left it. He goes back out and around the side. The mist has lifted somewhat, revealing another raccoon with its throat gashed.

When he returns to the house, he sees that the message light is flashing on the answering machine. His daughter called two days ago. She will not be coming home for the holidays this year. She and her new boyfriend are going away together.

He'll have to shut down her room, it appears. No use wasting heat on an unused space. The house is an empty cave. Beside the sofa and the kitchen, what need does he have for all these rooms? Why, he can't even take a bath.

The farmer picks up the telephone and looks up his daughter's number.

"Hello," she says.

"Hello," he says.

"Who is it?" she says.

"Hello," he says.

"Hi dad," she says.

She asks him if he received her message. He tells her he did and that he will be closing the vents to her room and is thinking of doing the same for his own bedroom.

"Where will you sleep?" she asks.

He says on the living room sofa. He doesn't tell her about his stiff neck. Just that he usually nods off on the sofa after supper, before the news comes on…

"Dad," she says. "Have you been watching the news at all?"

"Not much. TV's often on, but I can't make out what they're talking 'bout most the time."

"Dad, haven't you heard the about what just happened? It's all over the media."

"What is?"

She tells him. She tells him what has happened. All the hubbub about the signals and stuff. Intelligent life. How the discovery may be, like, the greatest of all time.

"Sounds exciting," he says.

"I'm amazed you haven't heard about any of this. People have been going crazy. Imaginations are running wild about the aliens."

"Mm. I can just imagine."

"So nothing unusual has happened out at the farm?"

"Well, I found a couple of dead 'coons near the shed. Seems I'm not their only enemy."

"Raccoons? Really? Did a dog attack them?"

"I haven't seen any trace of a dog anywhere. Probably something feral. I just don't know of any animals round here big enough to kill a 'coon, except maybe a wolf. 'Course nobody's seen a wolf in these parts for years. But you shoulda' seen the job it did on those 'coons. Tore the throat right offa' them."

"Okay, dad," she interjects. "I get the idea. How about a wild cat, like a lynx? They live in the area. Maybe there's one lurking around the farm."

"Sure, maybe," he says. What he doesn't add is: Could it be there's one big enough to rip apart a tractor and swallow a truck, too?

She tells him a little more about her holiday plans and says she is sorry she will miss him this year. "Maybe I'll be able to swing by after New Years," she says.

"Yeah, maybe," he replies. There is a pause, and then he says, "And how's your mother doing?"

"Oh, the same."

"Adjusting to the new apartment all right, is she?"

"Pretty well, I guess, all things considered."

Another awkward pause. Then he says, "Okay honey, well you have a good trip. I'll see you as soon as you can come down."

"Oh, dad, she says, I'm not going away just yet. I'll call you again before then."

"Okay, dear. Well, you take care."

They hang up. He stands in silence for a moment and then goes to her bedroom. Only a few of her old possessions remain: some records, some costume jewelry, some books she didn't take with her. He opens her closet door.

The closet is almost empty except for a box filled with old toys and clothes. Next to it is a small bookshelf containing a child's encyclopedia set.

He pulls out the volume labeled LA to LY and flips through the pages. Eventually, his eyes settle on an entry. They peruse it over and over:

> **LYNX** (Pr. *links*. Pl. **Lynx or lynxes.**) Short-tailed wildcats with tufted ears and soft, thick fur; of the genus *Lynx,* such as *L. canadensis* or *L. lynx.* Known for hunting small rodents, birds, and raccoons…

*   *   *

The news really was everywhere. Within days, cable media networks lit up with talk about the 61 Virginis-e. CNN's crawlers flashed the words Mylar, Signals, Not Alone, and Emissions about every 90 seconds. Rachel Maddow openly queried whether US immigration policy could adequately accommodate this new interstellar demographic. On Fox, businessmen, Sunday school teachers, and evangelists debated about the implications of the discovery for the Democratic party's next presidential run. Stories about beheadings, mass shootings, drone attacks, celebrity rapists, superstorms, and the NFL playoff run disappeared from people's TV screens. It was as if the world suddenly lost interest in itself. All anyone wanted to hear about were those mysterious signals emanating from across a dark ocean nearly twenty-eight light years wide.

The online media was aflame as well. On Twitter, the most popular hashtags were #Lexxeigh, #Mylar, #VirgoMylar, #Myfavoritevirgins.com. On Facebook, Lexxeigh was receiving more friend requests than Shakira, and she didn't even have a FB account. The Guardian posted a couple articles about her fashion preferences, and suddenly everyone was wearing denim. Even Kanye West, whose top ten hip-hop hit, "28 F*cking Lt Yrs Away," included a 20-second sample of the 61 Virginis transmissions. His wife, however, wasn't faring as well. It seemed that no one cared about Kim's butt anymore. It had become eclipsed by an even more exotic celestial object.

The Discovery Channel was now the post popular network on cable. Syfy ran a 24-hour marathon of all four *Space Odyssey* films for over a week. Netflix began offering every first contact B-movie ever made, including *First Contact, Star Trek: First Contact, Contact, The Day the Earth Stood Still, Close Encounters, Independence Day, Alien* 1, 2 and 3, *Invasion of the Neptune Men, Plan 9 from Outer Space, Battle: Los Angeles, War of the Worlds* (both the 1953 and 2005 films), and *Alf.* Overnight, the ratings for *X-Files* on the streaming network jumped from 58th place to 3rd, ironically right behind *Californication* and just ahead of the *Fresh Prince of Bel Air.* Disney announced it would be starting production of a fourth *Star Wars* trilogy, this one telling how Earth first discovers and then conquers the Galactic Empire, and George Lucas finally assumes his rightful place as Universal Overlord.

As for the woman behind this, the Greatest Discovery Ever, well, it's hard to say how all this attention was affecting her. At the initial press conference, which, at the behest of her professors, she reluctantly attended, a reporter asked her whether she was pleased with her findings. To everyone's amazement, she said she was pretty disappointed. She really expected to find a few moons out there. The reporters laughed, having no recourse but to assume she was joking, offering an example of that dispassionate detachment and irony her generation was famous for. But Lexxeigh did not join in the merriment. She merely smiled weakly, then excused herself, saying she had some more calculations to attend to, then handing the microphone over to her professors to finish the conference.

But someone else was also experiencing some serious dysphoria over Lexxeigh's discovery at the time. You see, only two weeks before, another major scientific event had merited the acclaim of being, like, the greatest thing that's ever happened. A team from the European Space Agency, led by Dr. Sebö Kecskeméti, had sent a probe to 2 Pallas, one of the largest asteroids in the solar system. The probe had landed on the asteroid's surface about a month before, and a couple weeks later, a rover sent from the probe confirmed that soil samples showed evidence of the presence of Psilocybin. The rover then found the source of the compound: a patch of mushrooms clinging to a rock on the shady side of a large crater. The first evidence of extra-mundane life in the universe turned out to be 'shrooms.

Within hours, Kecskeméti had become a virtual household name, and people wearing ESA tie-dye tees could be seen in every public facility known to humanity, from football stadiums to museums to concert halls. A meme showing a beaming, godlike Kecskeméti standing atop a rocky moonscape under the words "There's a Fungus Among Us" raced around the internet at light speed. *People* magazine included him among its top 50 Sexiest Men, and even *Time* indicated he would be in the running for Person of the Year.

But then it all came apart. Eight days later, this upstart grad student vegan hipster from the U.S. west coast upstaged him with what can only be considered the Ultimate Prize of Astrophysics. The discovery of an extra-terrestrial mushroom simply cannot compete with that of an advanced civilization. Suddenly, it was like the Beatles Invasion was happening all over again, and this Hungarian Frankie Valli was finding himself relegated to the status of Sebö Who? The humiliation couldn't have been greater. Twenty years of careful preparation and studious intent swept aside in an instant by some flakey hippy chick who probably still possessed all her old Pokémon cards.

To put it simply, Kecskeméti was pissed. He brooded all day in Buda and all night in Pest. He would spend long evenings pacing the Danube's East Bank beneath the skeletal frame of the parliamentary Országház, muttering Ugric invectives at this girl he didn't know and had never met but who had so obviously launched herself into the pantheon of Discoverers *by accident*, who may or may not be a little witch, some miserable *Jezinka* who threatened to tear away not only the light from his eyes but the soul they housed, but who was more likely than not just another upstart flash-in-the-pan twit, an amateur she-goat wannabe with little intellect and even less academic potential, scarcely worthy of his, or the world's, attention.

Then he got a look at her picture.

*   *   *

Shimon is looking at his reflection in the water and suspiring like a furnace.

No one can say why. These were supposed to be his salad days. The bakery is thriving. The challah has been hopping off the shelves, the new chocolate hamentaschen are a hit, and Mordechai, the grocer, has given him a discount on pareve flour. His twelve children, ages four to nineteen, are all healthy and fit as fiddles. His eldest, Yakov's bride Aliya, can braid dough like nobody's business, and Yakov's precocious command of numbers indicates he will soon be able to oversee the books. Leah remains a good and faithful wife and doesn't noodge him about his sweat stains so much as she used to. She even bought herself a new sheitel that makes her look a little like Mary Tyler Moore in her prime. Not bad.

So why does his gut feel like it's been glutted with pork loins?

When he was a young man, about 13 or 14, and doubt clouded his heart, he would play a little game with himself. He would take out the little pocket Torah his grandfather gave him for his bar mitzvah and, with his eyes pressed shut, open it to a random page and point to a word. Then he would ruminate on the word for a while. In one instance, the word that turned up was *natan*, which means to give, and so he decided that he was to offer something of himself, perhaps to be more selfless and generous. On another occasion, his finger landed on *lev*, the word for heart, which yielded a whole constellation of associations leading from love to courage to the core of his very being.

Today, he tried the game again. His finger landed on the word *coch'vim*. Stars. From the passage in Genesis, where Ha-Shem blesses Abraham and promises to multiply his seed like the stars of heaven.

Shimon looked at the word for several minutes. Then he went to the bathroom, leaned over the sink, and emptied out the contents of his stomach.

And so he is here now, immersed in the waters of the Brentwood Jewish Center's mikvah, in duteous acquiescence to the need to wash the despair off his flesh. So far, it hasn't worked. He still suffers from nausea, though it's obvious the source isn't medical, neither dietary nor gastronomical. It's more like what the gentiles call anguish. A sense of total alienation from the forces of causality and effect. A disillusionment of the heart and a dissolution of self into pure abstraction. An intense feeling of isolation, even loneliness, coupled with the peculiar desire to remain alone.

But he is not alone. For in comes Hebel Berkowitz, the cloth salesman, his sack-like belly sagging over his waistline like a deflated loaf of rye. Shimon watches with barely concealed dismay as the elder man eases himself into the water, displacing the surface by surely half a cubit.

After dipping his head underwater the requisite number of times, Hebel reaches for a towel. It is only after he has patted his eyes that they open widely, feigning sudden recognition.

"Shimon, is that you? I didn't realize!"

"Nice to see you, too, Hebel."

"The bakery must be doing well, you being here this time of day. You have my rugelach all ready, I trust?"

"Of course. How could I forget an order from one of my, er, biggest customers."

The men exchange pleasantries about business and their families for a moment or two. Hebel offers up some gossip about a cantor in the Bay Area who was caught having an affair with one of his students, and Shimon nods and shrugs as if to say, "This, too, is well known." That's when Hebel broaches the topic neither wants to mention, but which a condition of mutual nakedness seems to command the expression of:

"So you have heard the news, I take it?"

"Yes, unfortunately."

"It's a good thing I do not own a television set. Though in times like this, not having access to TV may not be so beneficial."

"Do you think it's a fabrication?"

"What, like what they said about the Moon Landing? Or the Holocaust?"

Both men immerse themselves at once. When they come up again, Shimon continues:

"You know that's not what I'm suggesting. I mean, do you think maybe they got their facts wrong? That they embellished them a little to, you know, save face."

"Who am I to speculate on these things? But the more important question is: What if they are not making it up? What would *that* mean? And what would it mean for...us?"

The two men sit in silence for a minute or two. Light from a passing police siren flashes through the windows overhead, briefly casting a reddish glow against the stone interior.

Shimon licks some moisture from his lips, then says: "Has anyone asked *him* yet what he thinks?"

"I was hoping to bring it up tonight after davening."

"Good. Then we will know once and for all what all this signifies."

"Let us hope so."

"How can you doubt it? This is Shneiderman, after all. The heir of Maimonides. This isn't just some shlumpy pickle grocer we're talking about."

Hebel nods obligingly, then steps out of the pool and picks up his towel. He wraps it gingerly around his stubborn midriff, before saying: "Let's just say, I suspect neither of us would be having this conversation in a ritual bathtub if we didn't harbor some doubt..."

*　　*　　*

To describe Reb Shmuel Shneiderman as having something of the supernal about him would be an understatement. To the tight-knit Hassidic community of north LA, he's a rock star of near-divine proportions. This dude isn't merely the heir of Maimonides, he's the heir of David himself, Ha-Shem's blessed anointed one. Of course, no one would dare say this out loud. Doing so would put at risk everything this community has worked toward for decades; indeed, that His People have been toiling away for since the days of the first exile. Mere superstition doesn't drive such restraint. Words have power; the Torah is a graphemic version of Creation. If you pester an architect by asking too many questions about the temple he's planning, he's bound to abandon the project. So why risk offending The Master Architect of the Universe by butting into His business?

Not that the rebbe is unaware of these musings. He wouldn't be true messianic material if he couldn't read his congregants' minds periodically, now could he? And yet any time a whiff of messianic fervor reaches his nostrils, he merely giggles and, eyes twinkling, will joke: "Oh yes, and just imagine the hosts of Israel waging war against Gog and Magog under the command of a fellow named Shneiderman!" And yet he doesn't outright deny the possibility, either. Because to do so would be just as hubristic as to assume its truth. The ways of Ha-Shem are a mystery to behold. You have to walk such a fine line when dealing with the Divine Plan.

Tonight, however, eyes that normally beam an angelical light look as dark and lifeless as charcoal. The rabbi displays none of his usual winsome effervescence as he leads the hundred or so men in evening prayers. Instead, his carriage seems limp, his body language condemned to say something along the lines of, *We should all go out to McDonalds afterwards and order cheeseburgers, and why not? We're all screwed anyway.* And yet before Shimon or Hebel or any of the others have a chance to ask the question that has been chafing their tongues all day, he already has his reply in hand, taking a small book from his inside coat pocket and reciting the verse from Judges in which the prophetess Deborah sings about Meroz, which the Talmud interprets to be a star or a planet, and the accursed inhabitants of that world—before collapsing onto the bema like a ragdoll dropped from a child's hand.

When he comes to, the rebbe looks up into Shimon's solicitous eyes and asks: "Friend, is it true you have a van?"

"Why yes," says Shimon. "Do you think we should go to the hospital?"

"No," says Shneiderman. "Much further than that."

"Further? How much further?"

"About 400 miles further. Due North."

*   *   *

Everywhere you go these days, people are speculating about the Virgo aliens. Whether they are like us or different from us. Whether they have four limbs or eight or sixteen or none. Do they shop at something like a Trader Joe's? Maybe they're really hot. People have even given them a sexy name: The Virgonians, like some mythical people Odysseus might have visited, a race of beautiful men and women with exotic powers and strange religious rites. As a result, about half the population starts having more sex, while the other half, scared that the end of the world is nigh, practice total abstinence. Accordingly, birth rates will remain totally stable nine months later.

The Institute meantime has quickly amassed its best and brightest to analyze the shiploads of data streaming in. Kenny, Benny, and Ram are tasked with running spectroscopic tests on the planet's atmosphere. The results are encouraging, and meritorious of spontaneous if somewhat hyperbolic displays of high fives and fist pumps. Both absorption and emission spectra indicate a 3:1 nitrogen-oxygen ratio, only slightly higher than Earth's. There is an abundance of Hydrogen, indicating the strong likelihood of the presence of water. The carbon levels also indicate that the world could bear shelves of rock and soil the size of continents.

The team has also enlisted Dr. Rachel Heck, one of Stanford U's top semioticians, to study the signals' linguistic components. More Velma Dinkley than Diana Prince, Rachel is nevertheless an academic superstar in her own right, her work tracing the evolution of the voiced fricative in early Indo-European consonant enunciation having won numerous nominations for a National Humanities Gold Medal. She quickly confirms that the signal patterns appear to demonstrate several universal traits of systemic communication, including phonology, morphology and syntax and bear the critical properties of productivity, recursivity and displacement. The phonological and morphological aspects should be easy enough to identify and isolate; but it may take a little longer to figure out how these elements come together to convey meaning. Still, she is hopeful they can produce at least a preliminary translation in time for this year's MLA conference.

But Kenny is skeptical. All this linguistics talk is Greek to him. Maybe he just isn't sufficiently practiced in speaking to women with advanced degrees in the Humanities. Even ones who minored in computational linguistics. Or maybe it's just that however impressive her credentials, she is no Lexxeigh Mylar.

And just where is that sapphiric, denim-donning darling of the Space-Age 2.0 press and resurgent social media? The trouble is, no one really knows. After declining offers to dine with the US President, the Canadian PM, the UK Monarch, the President of France, the Prince of Monaco, and especially the President of Russia, she seems to have entered some sort of state of publicity remission. She has turned down interviews with every major news publication in the country, including *Vice*. She has even stopped tweeting. Her presence in the twittersphere, as in the material world, has been reduced to a bizarre sequence of re-tweets and rumor, with some speculating that she has been promoted to a high-level position at NASA, while the more conspiratorially minded wonder if she hasn't been abducted by government agents and conveyed before a panel of interrogators from the Interplanetary Phenomenon Unit in a subterranean room somewhere beneath Area 51. Whatever the case, she seems to have become a silicon copy of a carbon copy of a facsimile of her former, indomitable, indivisible Self.

If you told her all this, she probably wouldn't deny it, either. The truth is, of late, she has been behaving like someone who feels slightly superfluous and disjointed, like a word indiscriminately set off by question marks in an otherwise normal declarative sentence. She spends most of her days sleeping in and her evenings subsisting on takeout edamame and vegan stir-fry, reading marginally competent online confessional poetry and the promotional blogs of unrepresented artists. She sits for hours editing her journal, which she saves in a protected folder on Google Drive, where she keeps her most private and personal reflections, like how stereotypes (e.g., vegan=hippy) seem to operate along the same principles as metonyms (parts for wholes), how equations can also work metonymically ($E=MC^2$, e.g.), as can abbreviations (e.g., exempli gratia), and that maybe that's how our brains are structured, as complex reductionistic metonym-manufacturing machines. In her most recent entry, she writes that she is considering dropping Astrophysics altogether and writing poems about birds and insects and cauliflower instead.

But back at the Institute, the work of discovery continues. Data keep coming in, and though most of it is the same, some of it is not. Kenny's job is to collect the data and to note any variations or discrepancies. There are almost never any discrepancies, but sometimes there are variations. Sometimes a variation may look like a discrepancy, and so he has to determine whether it is truly a discrepancy or just a variation. Sometimes a discrepancy may look like a variation, and he will have to determine whether it is truly a variation or just a discrepancy. Usually it is not. Usually it is a variation. They don't receive a lot of discrepancies.

When he finds a discrepancy, and it is confirmed not to be just a variation, he notes it. He makes a note of it in a Word document stored in the Institute database, under the title Discrepancies. Discrepancies should not be mistaken for anomalies. Anomalies are recorded in another folder altogether, entitled Anomalies. There is no way you can mistake an anomaly for a discrepancy, or a discrepancy for an anomaly, if you record them separately like this.

There are no anomalies. There never are any anomalies. The Anomaly folder so far is empty.

"What if we get an anomaly?" Rachel asks. "What if we get an anomaly and don't recognize it for one? Would we be able to recognize an anomaly? Especially as we haven't got one before?"

"We would recognize it," he assures her. He is sure of this. He is an experienced discoverer, after all.

"But what if we get one and we don't recognize it?" she persists. "Maybe we already have received one, and we took it for a discrepancy. Shouldn't we check all the discrepancies to make sure we didn't miss an anomaly?"

"We didn't miss any, he says. If we missed one, we'd know."

"How would we know? How? How?"

"He doesn't answer. He shouldn't have to respond to her questions at all. She's just a crazy Humanities scholar and has no understanding of the rigid standards of scientific method and observation. If only she might get sucked up into some anomaly and disappear."

"I'm going to look through all the discrepancies," she says. "I just want to be sure we didn't mistake any anomalies for discrepancies."

"You might as well check your variations, too," he says.

"Good idea," she says.

*　　*　　*

Another sleepless night. By 2:30 AM CET, having given up all hope of not being awake, he tosses off the blankets, throws on his day clothes and his overcoat, and steps out into the darkness. Turning his collar against winter's early advent, he moves in that methodical, agrypnotic, semi-dreaming manner of the hyper-caffeinated, down through the cavernous Paulay Ede, then along József Atilla past Erzsébet Square as far as Dorottya, before turning southeast, passing the still-occupied cafés with their barren summer patios, the cocktail bars and grills that demarcate the transition to Váci, the throbbing aorta in the center of District V, teeming with its famous bistros and boutiques (H&M, Zara, Esprit, Rolex, Foot Locker, the Hard Rock Café) and all the kids cluttering the cobblestone paths in exodus from the clubs and pubs, the rockers and the rappers and the hipsters, and every girl donning denim under her coat, hair fringed blue and eyes gleaming like moonstones.

Hours before sunrise, snowflakes start to fall like the remains of a shattered constellation. He enters a pub to warm up, approaches the bar, and orders a lager. A young couple huddles in a booth across the way. That could be him, twenty years ago, fresh from university and eyes enormous with ambition. And she, well, she could be...*his daughter.* The two of them sit there in a wordless reverie, like the romantic leads in a silent movie. They don't have to speak, or revert to a dependence on language to express what is so obvious to anyone who sees them like this: They are happy.

There was a time when all that mattered to him was work. Work is good. It's good to work. Working keeps the mind focused. Focused on work. There is much work to do. There is much to focus on. Keep working. Stay focused.

Work keeps the mind from drifting to other things. To other things in other places. Things and places half a world away. Worlds half a galaxy away. She has no idea who he is. That he, too, is a great discoverer. He's texted her like a thousand times, but she hasn't answered even once. All she's interested in is the work. The work that's its own reward. That's its own justification. The work that doesn't need any validation. It validates itself. Because it is good.

He is like a tiny man trapped in a bottle. A prisoner of the chambers of his own heart.

Shortly after sunrise, he receives a text. It's not from her. It's from a colleague. The tone announcing the arrival of the text, mingled with the subsequent disappointment, reverberates like a death knell for three or four minutes.

It's decided. He must do something. He has to say something. He must tell her, or he will fall apart.

But first, he has to tell his wife.

*   *   *

"It's because I'm fat, isn't it?" she shouts in their language. The language of Attila, of Bartók and the Gabor sisters. In the shrill and dulcet strains of a Ligeti concerto, a tongue of shimmering, shattered glass.

"No," he says. "I never said that."

"It's because I'm fat. It's not my fault I'm fat. It's not my fault father left mother when I was twelve. I was on the cusp of adolescence. It was a very impressionable age. I could have gone either way. But then he left her for a younger woman. A young, skinny woman. So I went this way. Is it my fault I'm so fat?"

"You're not fat. I never said…"

"Then what is it? You don't love me anymore? Is it my fault I'm so fat no one can stand me? Even my own husband, the big shit discoverer, wants to ditch me for some skinny stargazer."

"I don't understand, says a small voice in the next room. If people don't want to be fat, why don't they just go to the gym?"

"Zsófia, please. Grandma and Grandpa are having an argument."

"Do you want to hear me play Jingle Bells on the piano? Listen."
Plink-plink-plink, plink-plink-plink, plink plink plink, plink-plink.
"Who said anything about ditching you?" he asks.
"You plan on marrying her, don't you?"
"I never said—"
"Of course you want to marry her. Father married his skinny bitch. Now you want to marry yours."
"Is grandpa getting married?"
"Please Zsófia, not now."
"Why don't you go back to your piano, dear?"
"Okay."
Plink-plink-plink...
"I bet she's clever, too. Is it my fault I'm not clever?"
"But you are clever."
"Oh sure, you're just saying that because I'm fat."
He sighs. It's beginning to look like it wasn't a good idea to tell her.
"I'm not going to marry her, he says. I haven't even talked to her yet."
"You aren't? You haven't?"
"No. And all I want to discuss with her is work."
"That's it? Just work?"
"That's it."
"Ha! And to think he expects to seduce her just by talking about work. You obviously don't know a thing about women."
Plink-plink-plink....

*   *   *

By mid December, Rachel Heck announces to the team that she has made an important breakthrough. After accounting for all possible variations, not to mention any discrepancies and anomalies, she has not only verified that the signals originate from a highly sophisticated intelligent species and are being transmitted by advanced technological means, but as far as their meaning and purpose are concerned, she has narrowed down all possible variables to just two: either they represent an advertisement for some sort of alien coffee brand or a marathon broadcast of a performance of the galaxy's longest opera. This, after careful reflection, eliminated a third, albeit equally compelling, possibility.
"What is that?" asks Ram.
"That they are military communications related to a campaign to overthrow the galaxy."
"Oh my," says Ram.
"Wow, says Benny Chan. Thank goodness for that."
The team heaves a spontaneous gasp in amazement. This is also an expression of their collective appreciation of the historic importance of this moment. Their findings will soon draw worldwide attention and fill newsfeeds everywhere. The Institute will be the touchstone, gauge, yardstick and Polaris for all extra-terrestrial observation for years to come. The grant money will be pouring in by the bucketful.

In the background, the annoying synthesized signal motif introducing Pink Floyd's "Astronomy Domine" is pulsing through somebody's Bluetooth speaker, but no one seems to care.

Benny Chan dreams aloud about the new Nintendo 4D he's going to buy with his Christmas bonus. Ram starts whistling the melody of the Sleigh Ride song. Everyone is in good cheer, except, oddly, Rachel.

"What's the matter," asks Kenny. "You should be over the moon. Multiple moons, in fact."

"It's nothing," Rachel says.

"Come on," says Kenny, "let it out. You look like someone just died. No one has died, have they?"

Rachel shakes her head. Then she explains her dilemma. Her boyfriend has asked her to go to Tahoe with him for the holidays. She told him yes, but she has mixed feelings. There's the work, for one. And her family, for another. Her father and mother are split, and her father, who lives on a farm up north, will be all alone this year. She's worried about him.

Ram, who has been to Tahoe only once, during a fieldtrip in the seventh grade, and never, EVER with a girl, doesn't understand the problem. "I say go for it," he says.

"How long have you been seeing this young man?" Benny asks.

"Only a month."

"A month? Ay caramba!"

"No kidding," says Rachel. "He says he wants to take our relationship to higher ground. The trouble is, I'm not sure I'm ready to be in a serious relationship."

"I don't think this is about taking a relationship to higher ground," says Ram. "I think he's asked you to go to Tahoe with him because he wants to have sex with you."

"That's what I mean," says Rachel. "I don't ordinarily have sex with men unless I'm serious about them. I'm just not sure there's much of a future for us."

"What's holding you back?" asks Benny.

"Well," says Rachel, "We're not that intellectually compatible, for one. I met him in a fitness class in town. He's the instructor."

"A fitness instructor," says Ram. "So is he, like, impeccably fit?"

"Impeccably. His pecs are impeccable."

There is a silence, and then Ram says: "Then I think you should start thinking about getting serious about the dude…"

I don't understand. How did you get my number?

I told you. Your professor gave it to me. I explained that I work for the ESA, and needed to discuss something urgent with you..

If it's so urgent, why didn't you write to me?

I tried, but you will not answer my texts.

Well I'm answering them now. So go ahead and tell me already.

Please, I am here now. I flew a long way to see you. Can I please meet you in person? Besides, I cannot be sure this is a secure connection, and I do not want to risk our communication being intercepted.

You sound like a spy. Are you sure you aren't a spy? Or a creep?

I am not a spy. And I am not a stalker. I assure you, I am from the ESA, and I only want to discuss something very important about your work.

What work, exactly? I'm not doing much work at the moment, except writing some poems about carrots. Do you like carrots?

Not especially.

That's too bad. Okay, look: There's a nice little vegan café just to the east of the campus, near High and Hamilton. You can meet me there at noon. I hope you like other vegetables.

I will be fine with water. Thank you.

Do you need directions?

I will Google the way. Thanks.

Route 101 is moving with the celerity of a slow-rising loaf. All this humanity; honestly, it would have taken less time to lead the children of Israel across the Sinai, and back. Californians, it seems, have taken the commandment to go forth and multiply a little too literally. How can a country so vast, which could easily embrace a hundred Promised Lands, be so crowded? You can't even take a drive into the desert without running into a traffic jam. And yet they mock the Hassidim for being too fertile.

The passenger beside him is snoring like a bear. To think, this is how a messiah sounds when he sleeps. Somehow, you would expect a more graceful performance from someone born in a cradle carved by angels. Or is this the soundtrack to a sleep imbued with visions of chariots and seraphs and flaming swords? He's human, yes, and humans are fallible, and yet coming from someone of his stature, such noise seems so superfluous, so New Testament. Like the sequel or postscript to a story nobody asked for.

He hasn't spoken about The Question the whole trip. They've talked about flour and dough and recipes for piroshki, but not about That. It's hard to read the blessed man's reticence. Is it a reflection of his courage or his doubts? There's no telling what effect the current crisis, with all its theological and teleological implications for the covenant and its adherents, could be having on him. At best, it has brought him, and their community, closer to the Will of Ha-Shem. At worst, well, that would be unthinkable. At worst, he will be proven to be no better than the rest.

And yet it is impossible to avoid the issue outright. What if it is true, what they are reporting? There could be no Jews, no Pious Ones, out there; or could there? *And all the days of Enoch were three hundred and sixty-five years; and Enoch walked with God, and he was not, for God took him.* Where did He take him? Could Enoch have been transported to another planet? Is such a thing beyond His power? And what of Elijah, swept up in a blazing chariot and carried off like Dorothy in a whirlwind? Where did that chariot land? And what untold worlds did he possibly visit and share and disseminate the Torah with, out there in the heavens?

These are the musings of a pious spirit, nourished on the creative exegetics of the Midrash, when confronted with something new and, until now, unthinkable. Or they are the philosophical reflections of a madman.

The traffic, which has been moving at a steady 20 mph for the past fifteen minutes, slows to another standstill, prompting the rebbe to stir with a snort. He shakes his head briefly before beholding the barren topography outside his window. He predicts aloud that they have made some progress in their journey since he dozed off, and that they should be approaching Salinas momentarily. His driver nods, having no heart to tell him that they only just passed King City, and that even if the gridlock clears, Salinas will still be over an hour away.

*   *   *

Xoxoxo...
Xoxoxo...
"Wait!"
"What is it? "
"Sorry, I just can't turn off my thoughts."
"Is it work again? You deserve to take a break."
"I know, I know. Look, it isn't only that. I'm just not so sure we're suited for each other. I mean, you've got amazing pecs and all, but still..."
"But what? I'm not an intellectual colossus, is that it?"
"Well, no, but...I have to admit, I didn't think you knew words like colossus."
"Let me ask you something: these aliens of yours, what do you think they would do in our situation?"
"I—I don't know. I haven't gotten that far into my translation yet. "
"Do you think they would let anything like a little intelligent-quotient gap dictate whether two people are romantically suitable for one another?"
"I can't say whether they even have a notion of romance. Love is a pretty culturally determined thing."
"But it's also a many splendored thing. It's something that strikes wonder to the heart. It shocks, confuses, awes, and bewilders the mind and the spirit. Do you think the aliens have hearts?"
"I would suppose they possess some version of them, yeah."
"And do you think their hearts are filled with light and joy whenever they experience love? That their brains go dizzy with wonder and excitement?"
"Is that how you feel with...with me?"
"Sure. Now let me ask you something else. You say they're a pretty advanced race, right?"

"Exceptionally. The transmissions are very complicated. Yet they seem to talk on and on incessantly."

"Well maybe they're advanced in other ways, too."

"Like what?"

"Like anatomically, for example."

"Oh. Oh..."

"Imagine how those advanced bodies would look when their super-hearts are filled up with the splendor and radiance of love. Imagine what they would look like, together."

"Oh, yes. Yes!"

"Do you think their advanced brains would give a damn about intellectual compatibility under such circumstances?"

"Oh, I doubt there is any incompatibility up there."

"Prove it!"

"I will!"

Xoxoxo...

Xoxoxo...

* * *

The hub of bohemian Palo Alto is a little café in the back of a five story glassy industrial-looking building called the Veg for Lyfe Kitchen, about a fifteen-minute walk from the northeast corner of the Stanford campus. Here you will find the crème of the city's hippest plonked at a table, eyes appended to their laptop or a tablet reading an e-copy of the *I Ching* and enjoying a healthy serving of fresh fake chicken wings, garden burgers, tofu tacos, ancient grain bowls, Thai salads, kale salads, and edamame or guac & chips by the plateful, not to mention the free wi-fi. It's a hip hub. And it is here a certain lunar explorer-cum-literary-neophyte finds herself this evening. She should be celebrating the recent publication of her teeny tiny ode to Brussels sprouts, entitled *Brassica oleracea gemmifera*, in an online lit zine, or putting the finishing touches on her flash fiction piece about almond milk addiction, or poring through blogs about ugly Renaissance babies. But instead she is sitting here listening to a man twice her age go on and on in a barely intelligible foreign accent about disturbances and shock and panic and what sounds like an avouchment that he is not hitting on her.

"Listen, Sobo is it?"

"Sebö."

"That's what I said. Listen, I get it. You're not trying to seduce me. That's great, because I'm not really all that interested in being in a relationship right now. Especially with an older, central European man I can barely understand."

"What is it you do not understand?"

"What?"

"I said, what is it you do not understand?"

"Ugh. I wish there was another language we could use. You don't speak French by any chance?"

"*Mais oui.*"

"Terrific."

So they try French for a while, but she soon finds his French pronunciation is riddled with even more plosives and affricates than his English. She might as well be talking to a rusty lawnmower.

"Where do you say you're from again?"

"Budapest."

"Darn. I don't know any Hungarian. Can you give me a couple of weeks? I think I can master enough of the language's noun inflections by that time to give this another go."

But he insists there isn't time, that he must speak to her now. The matter is of the greatest urgency, and if they wait any longer it may be too late. She nods and lets her eyes wander to the table next to them. A guy with thick-rimmed glasses and facial hair and a girl with thick-rimmed glasses and no facial hair are seated there, engaged in some sort of conversation both appear to understand. The server, who wears neither thick-rimmed glasses nor facial hair, arrives with their food. They've both ordered the baby Buddha bowl with tempeh, artichokes, chickpeas, soba noodles, cashews, almonds, and peanut sprouts and a side of quinoa onions rings. The couple thank the server in unison and make idle chitchat with him. The server's facial expression falls somewhere on the spectrum between a throbbing spasm and sardonic irony. As though he finds the couple too irritatingly cute for words. As though he is about to run back to the kitchen and tell the cooks: "They eat the same food. They complete one another's sentences. They probably wear each other's underwear, too."

The server turns to the astrophysicists and asks the younger one if she is enjoying her bowl of macro greens. She nods and tells him it's delicious. He then asks the older one if he would like a refill of his mineral water, but the latter shakes his head and says he is fine.

After he departs, they sit in silence for a few minutes, like two people wishing they were living the lives of someone else right now. But it's then that they are approached by the pair of bearded men who have just entered the café. What distinguishes these men from the other bearded guys in the place is that, first, they are older, and second, they are wearing neither plaid nor sandals but white shirts with black vests, black wool jackets and trousers, and black felt hats, which would give them the vague appearance of pre-Enlightenment era penguins, except that their accents are totally SoCal.

"Excuse me, says the first man, but would you happen to be Miss Mylar, the scientist?"

"Oh my, she says. How—how do you know me?"

"Ah. Ha-Shem knows every one of His blessed creatures."

"Ha-Who?"

"So does Google, says the second man."

"Do you mind if we ask you some questions," asks the first man.

"That depends. What kind of questions?"

"Oh, nothing out of the ordinary. Just the usual stuff about the size and dimensions of the cosmos, and man's place in it."

"Whoa. That sounds pretty heavy."

"Not at all, says the second man. He's a holy man, can't you tell? Haven't you noticed he's levitatin?"

"No."

"Me neither."

"The cloyingly cute couple at the next table suddenly explodes into a fit of giggles. Undoubtedly the guy just told the girl a ridiculously unfunny joke or anecdote about something he encountered in his otherwise exceedingly inconsequential life. The girl laughs in a somewhat nervous way, probably because her own life is fairly empty and superficial too, and because she is convinced she loves him. That is, her attachment to him falls somewhere on the spectrum between sufferance and acceptance, like a chronic arthralgic who learns with time and patience and several dozen visits to the naturopath how to live with the pain seething through his joints.

The first bearded man pays them no mind, however, having launched into a rather lengthy defence against modern scholarship's attestation that the ancient Israelites received their god from the southern lands, that he was transported into the hill country by escaped slaves, not the children of Abraham, Isaac, Jacob, and Joseph, but Canaanites who fled Egypt in a time of marked economic decline, when Egypt was an aging empire losing its grip on power and uprisings in the provinces were commonplace; that all this took place centuries after the book of Exodus tells of the eponymous journey of Moses and his argumentative people; and that the earliest evidence of Ha-Shem's name outside the bible comes from an inscription found in the land of Media in today's Southern Jordan, where it appears somewhat like the tetragrammaton but was probably pronounced something more like the search engine Yahoo.

Lexxeigh nods blithely while stabbing a chopstick at some kale leaves in her bowl. She tells the man that she is familiar with all this, having audited a few courses in Near Eastern Studies in college. But it wasn't escaped slaves who imported YHWH into the early Israelite pantheon, she says; rather, something more organic probably took place, with one clansman marrying another and carrying his or her traditions with him/her, and merchants passing in and out of the country bearing their beliefs like wares. Culture doesn't happen in a vacuum, she says, and it doesn't breed in a desert; it doesn't have starts and stops but ebbs and morphs like a shore-less sea. Like language, there is no ground, there is no *it*, there is only meaning, or value, if you will, perpetually deferred. The first bearded man looks at her like he is staring into the unblinking face of foreign idol. But there was nothing casual about it, he counters; every stage was planned like the verse in a carefully composed epic. The man then says that despite attacks from every possible direction, from the Egyptians and the Assyrians and the Babylonians to the Greeks and the Romans, from the pogroms and the Nazis and the Arabs to the historians and archaeologists, Judaism has survived and thrived for over three thousand years. So why is he now so afraid of some little girl wielding chopsticks over a bowl of mixed vegetables? Lexxeigh shrugs and continues eating while her Hungarian tablemate, who has not been able to get in a garbled word in some time, buries his face in his hands and mumbles something like: "I am a stranger in a strange land."

"Oh dear," says Lexxeigh. "Do either of you happen to speak Hungarian by any chance?"

"The first bearded man looks imploringly at the second, who replies somewhat sheepishly: "Sorry. Besides English, we only know Hebrew and Yiddish."

The Hungarian man's face suddenly brightens. "Yid-dish," he says. "*Sprechen sie Deutsch, ja*?"

The second bearded man acknowledges that Yiddish does share a lot of common elements with Middle German, prompting the Hungarian man to expatiate in a rather emphatic High German about an imminent scientific crisis of vast proportions, practically spraying the table with his glottal CHs.

The first bearded man looks at the second bearded man, who shrugs, then says to Lexxeigh: "He is talking about these signals of yours."

"Yes," says Lexxeigh, "I gathered."

"You speak German?"

"A little."

"Then you understand that he says the signals are dying."

"No, that's not quite right."

"It isn't?"

"It's not the signals that are dying, she says. It's the people making the signals."

Then she swallows one more mouthful of kale and arugula, takes a quick quaff of green tea, and dashes out the front door into the moonless night.

*   *   *

As soon as she reaches the Institute, the worst is confirmed. The signals have stopped. Data from the latest spectroscopic tests are still preliminary, but they show a sharp drop in oxygen levels in the atmosphere around 61 Virginis-e and a sharp increase in noxious sulfuric gases. There is also evidence of substantial amounts of bromomethane, carbon monoxide, hydrogen chloride, and other toxic compounds. It's too early to tell what caused these sudden changes, whether they indicate acute seismic and volcanic or anthropogenic activity, or both. But right now, nobody is in the mood to look into it.

Rachel Heck won't learn any of this until after she gets back from Tahoe, wearing the engagement ring given to her by her fitness instructor and a glow primed to evaporate the minute she finds out how wrong she got it; that the signals Lexxeigh's tests first detected weren't operatic at all, though they were certainly tragic enough. But for Lexxeigh, the news has already started to metastasize inside her. This is what Sobo, or whatever his name was, had been trying to tell her all along. That his colleague, a linguist from the Sorbonne specializing in code decryption, had conducted a deep analysis of the transmissions, and was 99% certain they functioned as radio beacons. The people there were sending out distress signals to the universe.

And now they have stopped. Or more accurately, 27.9 years ago to the day, they stopped. Had they persisted another 0.1 years, they would have been around for Lexxeigh's own 28th birthday.

"Oh god," she gasps.

Kenny, Benny and Ram gather around her solicitously, but she pulls away. She hastens out of the room and down the corridor. Her footfalls echo for several minutes from the stairwell.

A song from Pink Floyd's *Final Cut* is streaming from someone's Bluetooth in the background.

"For Pete's sake," says Ram, what's with all the Floyd, anyway?

Must be one of the older technicians, says Benny. Unless Kenny has suddenly developed a taste for obsolete prog bands, he adds.

But Kenny isn't there. He has gone out to look for Lexxeigh, and after a brief search finds her sitting outside on the front lawn, her arms folded around her knees, the collar of her denim jacket high up around her ears. She is not crying or anything, just staring vacantly, in an almost dissociative way, into the night sky. A curtain of winter cloud has obstructed all celestial light, so that there is only a pervasive blackness, and the idea of a vast, undifferentiated oblivion. As if the heavens, too, have succumbed to the forces of obsolescence. Kenny gently whispers something to her, but she doesn't respond. Evidently she cannot hear him. Evidently he, too, is light years away, and just as silent. Ω

The Hzeen

Written By
Aaron Hamilton

Os panted, bent at the waist with his palms on his knees. He studied Mangijin carefully, knowing his tricks after years of sparring together. The creature chuffed in impatience, admonishing Os' fatigue while staring complacently through yellow eyes. Os rose to the balls of his feet with a deep breath, wishing that his opponent displayed the least sign of weariness.

"Finally." Mangijin's voice filled Os' mind, but he ground his teeth and wouldn't be baited. Os warily stalked forward, and the fine gravel barely crunched. His legs were long, but he had lost his gangly clumsiness within the last year, partially due to the torturous sessions with Mangijin.

Two tentacles lashed out toward Os, but he rolled beneath the menacing suction cups in time to deflect a third sweeping arm. A fourth rose, but he was already tucked and rolling backward as it puffed out sand meant to blind him. Mangijin writhed closer on his remaining arms, terrifyingly quick, eyes burning into Os'.

The chilling fear leaked through his eyes and mind and down into his spine. Os felt his arms and legs weaken with its creeping progress but used his panic to anger and heat him. He sprang forward, casting a handful of sand at the yellow orbs. Too slow, Mangijin slid sideways, easily avoiding the hazard. He pulled his tentacles beneath him, rose to an intimidating height, and disappeared.

Os slid to a halt, fighting to listen for shifting sand over his labored breathing. Mangijin had never before employed his natural camouflage during any of his lessons. Os reached out with his mind, groping for some sign of his teacher's presence. He knew Mangijin's eyes must be closed to hide, but the

Desert Fear were gifted telepaths, even without the blood of the Spire, and Os felt his opponent's senses upon him. It should have been impossible for him to move silently through the gravel, yet Os heard nothing.

The tentacle swept his legs at his ankles. Os tried to roll away, but the overpowering arm bound his legs together. Another coiled around his chest and trapped one of his arms. Mangijin revealed himself and slowly pulled Os toward a lethal beak the size of his foot. It was the last thing he saw before another tentacle wrapped completely around his head and began to squeeze.

Os raised his free arm desperately. Just as he spurted a spine from his wrist, the arm was slapped away.

"Chuffchuffchuffchuffchuffchuff," greeted his failure. "You are dead. I took my time about it and gave you several openings."

The pressure on his head blessedly eased, and the tentacle unwrapped from his face, smacking suction cups pulling at his cheek.

Mangijin held Os upside down from his legs and stared into the youth's eyes. "The spine was predictably clumsy. You should have used it earlier, before you tired."

"It takes time to prepare the secretions."

"Time you could not spare when you were always on the defensive. It was a desperate attempt. The sand was better, but still inadequate."

Os' legs were unexpectedly released. He tucked and landed on his feet but needed to roll over backward when he lost his balance. He couldn't help but take some satisfaction in avoiding a broken neck.

"Maybe if I had four extra limbs, I'd stand a chance against you." It left his mouth before he could stop it. Repeated losses had bruised his ego, but he felt shame at the outburst. Mangijin's reply exacerbated his embarrassment.

"These are lessons, not matches to be won or lost. What did you learn?" Mangijin's suction cups popped slightly as he tapped two tentacles together. It reminded Os of his human mother's fidgeting, somehow making the giant octopod less threatening.

"My breath control and physical conditioning are shameful. I hear but do not listen, relying too much on my vision. My mind is undisciplined and therefore weak. I attempt to anticipate my enemy's actions. Instead I should allow my training and instincts to guide me without thought." He phrased it as though from memories of Mangijin's many stern lectures over the last few years.

"You forgot to mention that you are an ungrateful and unworthy pupil." Mangijin let the scolding hang in silence for a moment. Os closed his eyes when he felt his exhaustion blurring his vision.

"I apologize, Master. I have much to learn." Os averted his gaze, hoping some additional respect might be answered with forgiveness.

"No. Today was your last lesson."

The gasping pain in Os' chest surprised him as his mind raced. Mangijin naturally sensed it even before Os' jaw dropped.

"I believe only experience can truly teach you more. That is, if you live long enough."

"So I'm ready to find the Hzeen and honor my father?"

"No. I do not imagine that will end well for you." The yellow orbs blinked. "Perhaps some time hunting in the wastes or assisting the Spire's scouts will see you prepared properly."

Os tried in vain to hide his disappointment.

"It calls to me nearly every time I sleep. I've seen it and the thieves who have it. I don't think they know what it is, yet they value its beauty." Os clenched his fists until his arms trembled. "They killed him. The Hzeen showed me."

"So you will honor your father by dying as he did? Do not walk that path, boy." Mangijin seemed to deflate a bit. The intensity faded from his eyes, but it only increased in his voice. "You can serve the Spire with honor, and years from now, when you have grown to your full potential, the Hzeen will still call to you."

"I dared the Midnight Tracks to fashion my spear. I claimed a scale from Chorpaneshi's children as my shield, and bled for my right to live within these walls. By these deeds, I am no boy." Os felt a knuckle pop as his fists tightened, and he calmed himself with some effort.

"I know the laws. You are a blood citizen of the Spire. Why do you still seek my advice when you know what is best? Go." Mangijin's scales flushed purple-red, and he pointed with one enormous tentacle toward the cavern entrance. "I have other pupils more deserving of my attention."

Mangijin slowly relaxed and faded into the background of the cave wall. Os winced and trudged away toward his meager quarters. The dismissal nagged at him, and he found himself turning away down another corridor toward yipping laughter. He felt his spirit lighten and quickened his pace, almost forgetting his exhaustion.

Sward lay on his belly in a disc of sunlight. He worked a long bone in his teeth as he held one end under an elongated, clawed hand. Occasionally he yipped at something privately amusing. Sward looked like one of the Snapjaw Clan that prowled the wastes after sundown. His body was humanoid with long-toed feet and short, sandy hair, but his neck was thick, and his head sloped down to a pointed snout, reminiscent of coyotes. The emerald palms of his hands revealed his shared ancestry with Os, but they were the only signs. A pointed ear turned toward Os' approach, but Sward's concentration never left the bone.

"By your laughter, I thought you had company." Os squatted a few paces away, knowing better than to get within an arm's reach of Sward's prize.

Sward gave the bone several calculated licks before raising his eyes to Os and letting his tongue loll between menacing teeth. "I was laughing at you, hairless." The chiding entered Os' mind abruptly, without the customarily gentle wordless greeting of the Silent Speech. "Your noisy feet tell a tale of failure, disappointment, and frustration." He pointed the bone at Os. "I notice that from a lot of Mangijin's pupils."

"Well it's the last time you'll notice it from me. I've been dismissed." He stared at the ground, not ready to meet Sward's eyes.

"Surprised you lasted as long as you did." The bone drew Sward's attention again for a moment, but Os sensed he wasn't finished. "Everyone thought you would quit long ago." Scrape, scrape against the bone. "I bet even Mangijin thought so, but he'd never say it to a student. If he couldn't make you quit, then he must think you're ready."

"No." Os drew a wavy pattern in the sand at his feet. "At least, not ready for what I need to be. I want to find the Hzeen of my father." The scraping stopped. Os looked up to see Sward looking at him with his full attention, head slightly cocked to the side.

"Do you think you're ready?" Now Sward gripped the bone in both hands as though they could break apart what his powerful jaws could not.

Os hesitated only a moment, but Sward's shoulders slumped, and he knew the canid had sensed his doubt. "I don't know. I feel strong enough, and I'm not afraid to fight. But Mangijin reminded me of my weaknesses."

"Mangijin feels it is his job to make his pupils feel weak. He crushes them with their failures." Sward's callused hands rasped against the bone as he wrung it. "The strongest tend to train harder to prove him wrong, like you did. The weaker quit. Some die, but some," tapping the bone against his hairy chest, "survive to spite him."

Os had few friends in the Spire. He told himself his human lineage was to blame, though there were other half-humans who didn't seem to earn the same resentment. Years of rule by human descendants had ended in the only internal strife in the Spire's history, well before Os had arrived. The children of humans had been deposed, and the last human Elder had died decades before his father's time. Os tried to gain respect through his courage and deeds, earning it by the Spire's laws, but it was given to him grudgingly. His father had claimed more than his share of accolades, but Os had never met him to learn what his life was like before he'd been accepted into the Spire. Sward didn't seem to care about Os' human mother, but Sward was a bit of an outsider himself.

"Tomorrow at dawn, I'm leaving to find the Hzeen." He stood, and Sward sprang to his feet as though challenged. Os instinctively leapt back, only to realize his mistake.

"Why not now? Wait, and Mangijin's doubts will have more time to haunt you."

"If I change my mind by the morning, then I'll know I'm not really ready. Besides, I want to drink from the cistern and spend a few hours in the sun before I wait to see the Elders." Os now stood only a pace from Sward, fully in the creature's shadow. Sward blinked down at him but didn't growl at his close proximity to the bone.

"Elders? As if they care. I will join you." The giant tongue lolled again.

"It will be nice to drink in company."

"Yes, and tomorrow we'll travel together to find your Hzeen."

Os blanched at the taboo Sward suggested, until he realized what would come.

"You'll pay your debt by helping me reclaim mine first." Sward released the bone to flex his right hand, the newer one with a slightly lighter palm. "You've told me yours is much further away."

Os had heard the tale of Sward's Hzeen and knew it had been lost, along with the hand that held it, in the last battle at Boiling Rift. Sward claimed his father's voice still called to him from the Hzeen. Some said the loss left Sward mad, and the way he howled on an occasional night left Os wondering if they were right. He knew Sward would be useful out in the wastes: a savage fighter with sharp senses and the endurance to run for a full day. Could he help Sward in turn? He would be bound to the task, even until death, if he accepted Sward's offer. To leave their ancestors' spirits in the Hzeens, surrounded by enemies, was a crime against them and all the Spiredwellers, but Os heard Mangijin's dismissal in his memory all too clearly.

"Tonight in the amphitheater, we declare our intentions."

"To the cistern then." Sward raised the bone to his mouth again and walked away toward the spiraling descent to their water source. Os followed the scraping of teeth on bone, anticipation already fluttering in his gut.

*   *   *

Peace normally fell across Os' mind when he submerged his feet in the cistern and stood with the sun in his face, but today's visit had done little to soothe him. The water tasted sweet as always, and the sun sent a wave of comfort through his eyes and down into his core. Some of the older Spire dwellers never awoke from their final drink, but Os drank with youthful exuberance, letting the water fairly gush into his pores. Sward, as always, seemed blissfully amused at one breath and bristling for a fight with the next. Eventually Os' worries subsided. Sward's occasional whines and yips faded. Os' thirst no longer nagged at him, and the flow from the cistern became sips in rhythm with his heartbeat. He let his thoughts run freely, trying to objectively consider Mangijin's advice.

The Spire was ancient, but the cistern was not. The progenitor of Os' people, Huxley, had dug it with his own hands after losing his way in the Waste. Making his way to the Spire, he had found shelter from sandstorms and received visions from Chorpaneshi, leading him to the water source. Blessed by the Immortal Excavator, Huxley had sown his seeds and bid his children to populate the Spire, to defend it, to leave their souls in the holy vessels, the Hzeens.

Os had never held the Hzeen containing his family's souls. His father had carried it on the trail of mutants, never to return. Os had made his way to the Spire too late to ever meet his sire or inherit the Hzeen. How much worse it would be to suffer its loss like Sward's.

Sward's voice interrupted Os' reflections.

"Having second thoughts?" When Os' eyes opened, the canid waded out of the water. He knelt at its edge and filled skins, watching the bubbles with his head cocked to the side.

"Not anymore." Os did the same with skins of his own. As the skins inflated, he gave thanks to Chorpaneshi, to Huxley, and to his ancestors. The daily assemblage of Elders always took place the hour before sunset. Supplicants massed in the largest cavern at ground level, known simply as the Gathering Hall. The Histories claimed the spacious hall had been the only room when the Spire was young. It had been gifted to them by Chorpaneshi's own excavations. Tremors from his passage could still be felt through the floor if one were blessed. The room rose perhaps ten strides high and one hundred in diameter, with narrow, vertical openings beginning twenty strides from the floor and reaching nearly to the ceiling. A packed earthen platform rose from the southwestern section, where the light of the setting sun could be felt by the Elders and those who approached to address them. Os and Sward waited their turns. Ahead of them shuffled or crawled a loose line of those with grievances to air or problems requiring the Elders' wisdom. Occasionally, another supplicant joined the line from among the smooth, irregular pillars. He could remember times when the Gathering Hall had been so crowded that Spire dwellers were forced to sit in darkness. Tonight they were few in number, though Os had tried to spread word of their intentions during the afternoon and early evening. All the better, he thought, because the Gathering Hall will be filled when we return with our Hzeens. Then a place of honor will be made for us next to the Elders, at least for one night.

He was unaccustomed to speaking to an audience of more than one, that one usually Mangijin or Sward. All day, he had rehearsed his simple speech and prepared himself for the possibility that he would be forbidden to embark on his journey. He closed his eyes and breathed himself calm, relying on his ears to tell him when the line moved forward. At last, his name was called in the Silent Speech. Before him his audience sat, opening their minds to his, waiting with mostly feigned interest. Mangijin was nowhere to be seen or felt.

"Respected Elders, brothers and sisters," Os began, "I come before you to make heard my intention to seek out and reclaim the Hzeen of my father." He paused, but when nothing was said he continued. "I will travel into the Waste with my friend, Sward." He waved a hand toward his companion. Unfortunately Sward's attention was elsewhere, but at least he no longer chomped his treasured bone. "In return, I will aid him in recovering his Hzeen, lost in the last battle at Boiling Rift. We leave after first light's prayers. May we carry Chorpaneshi's blessing." Os stood with bowed head and waited. Finally, a rich voice filled his mind, and he could hear Sward straighten to attention behind him. He knew it also reached out to touch all those in attendance. "Do you know where you head, boy?" The crest on the old lizard-man's head straightened then rested flat once more. Os hadn't expected a conversation, only a decision and ultimate dismissal.

"Yes, Elder Taznian. I have heard its singing for some time now. It is far from the Spire, and enemies surround it." Os tried to puff out his chest in defiance at the Elder's condescension, but the gesture met only indifference.

"You are too young to have sown your seeds. Who will avenge you when you die?" Taznian licked one bulging eye and continued before Os could respond. "Much as we hate any Hzeen to remain lost, let alone be corrupted by the hands of the ruinous horde, you endeavor only to waste your life. But it is yours to waste. I knew your father, and he was brave and foolish like you. Go with Chorpaneshi's blessings. Return with honor and newfound wisdom." A clawed hand waved him away. The assents of the other Elders followed him and Sward as they left with doubts echoing in their minds.

*   *   *

Most of the Spire dwellers were drawn to sleep once darkness came since the seeds that had spawned them inextricably married them to the sun. Some, especially the young and those with nocturnal ancestors, could resist the instinct to enjoy the world lit only by moon and stars. Such were Os and Sward, both normally serving among the Spire's evening force of guards. As was customary, that night they were left to rest before their journey, but Os could not quiet his mind. He spent hours in contemplation of his training with Mangijin, listening to the call of his Hzeen and remembering the story of the battle that had claimed Sward's.

Three years had passed, time enough for Sward to grow a new hand with the help of the sun. Hardly a scar remained where his hand and wrist had been severed by the Riftborn, but Sward bore other scars that would only be healed once he again grasped his Hzeen. The small Riftborn typically traveled far from their birthplaces, hoping to establish new colonies and grow fat on the weak and unwary. These Os killed by the score with spear and shield and even his hands at any opportunity. They were nothing compared to those who defended the Boiling Rift itself. Those monsters wore carapaces that could turn teeth, claws, and spears, and they boasted jaws that could dismember an unlucky foe with ease. Sward could attest to that.

Frustrated as sleep continued to elude him, Os wandered as if drawn to the Hall of Ancestral Light. The green glow served as the only illumination, forcing Os to squint until his eyes acclimated. Mounted on the wall were all of the Hzeens without living heirs. Once he had tried to count them, only to lose track in the shifting light and the distraction from so many eager voices. Occasionally a bond would form between the spirits in one of the vessels and a Spiredweller, and the Hzeen would be taken from the wall to arm a new champion. Os personally knew no one to have claimed such an honor, though there were plenty of accounts in the Spire's history. Most, like he, came to bask in the glow and pray for guidance from the most revered among the ancestral souls.

"Ravnid's was always my favorite." Os turned to see Elder Taznian approaching. "I have spoken with him many times, as he is generous with his guidance when I lack wisdom." Following Taznian's gaze, Os looked upon a glowing Hzeen as wide as his head. Its shape was two half-moons, joined by a central handle darkened by use.

"He must have been huge to wield a Hzeen of that weight." Os knew Ravnid's reputation as a warrior.

"Yes," agreed Taznian, "especially for one born of a human. Now he fights no more. He considers no one worthy to carry his Hzeen, but he still gives good advice when I need to make a difficult decision."

"I still have trouble hearing individual voices," Os confessed, "but if I quiet my mind, they seem to blend together almost like song." He stood and faced Taznian. "Have you and the Council changed your minds about my quest with Sward?"

"No, no, nothing like that. Have you?"

"No, Elder. I just can't sleep and hoped this would help. At least these will be my last memories of the Spire before I leave."

"Ravnid thinks you have fire in you, Os. He sees you holding your Hzeen, dark with the blood of our enemies. One day he believes a mutant will be born who will eat the souls in every Hzeen it finds, until none of us remains in body or spirit."

"I will not fail, Elder. We will reclaim Sward's Hzeen and then my father's."

"With Chorpaneshi's blessings, you will."

Os watched Taznian shuffle out. With one last attempt, Os reached out to Ravnid, focusing all of his thoughts on the old warrior's Hzeen. After minutes without a response, Os thanked the multitude of souls in the Hall and walked back to his room.

*   *   *

Dawn lit their faces as they prayed. After filling water skins and gathering supplies and weapons, they ran toward the Waste. Os felt a steady fear creeping into his belly as the Spire shrank behind them. For four years he had lived and learned there, but it had never been a home to him. Leaving his mother behind to find the Spire had been much more terrifying, but the Spire was part of him, as it had been part of his father. To live without his Hzeen was to live without him.

They ran at a brisk pace, but occasionally they spotted signs of other travelers or possible threats which they carefully investigated. Sward's kind could run all day at a steady lope, and though Os was used to intensive exercise, he was grateful for the breaks. While they drank and allowed the sun to nourish them, Os took the opportunity to communicate his concerns about leaving the Spire.

"Perhaps you're too young for this." Sward allowed himself a few habitual chomps on his bone. "Time to grow up and be a warrior, I say. The sun tastes sweetest out here where the wind and sand can scour you. You'll see, once your spear drinks and your Hzeen rests in your grasp. You may never go back." Then he took off at a run, forcing Os to sprint to catch up. The wind felt fine indeed.

Later in the day, Os lagged behind. It seemed Sward had forgotten his friend as they entered deeper into the sun-blasted and dangerous Plain of Thirst. The Boiling Rift still hid behind rocky up-thrusts to the northeast, perhaps a day's travel at their current pace. Sward's enthusiasm drove him fearlessly onward. Finally Sward slowed and fell to all fours, tail wagging slightly. Os slowed as much as he dared, but he feared what his friend's formidable senses might have detected. He approached the last 100 strides in a crouch with his shield on his arm.

"What?" It was all Os dared to communicate for risk of revealing his irritation.

Sward turned his head and cocked it to one side. "Of course, you can't smell them. Down there in the creases in the earth," he pointed, "they're being killed."

"Who?" Os squinted.

"Snapjaws. The sand striders have them scared. I smell the fear."

Os hid his own shiver at the mention of the predators.

"Good, we don't want trouble from either of them." Os drank a greedy gulp from his skin. "We can find a way around their skirmish."

If the Snapjaws were traveling during the day, they were desperate or looking for trouble.

"Afraid, young Os?" Sward didn't wait for an answer. Once more, Os ran to keep up.

Ahead, the Snapjaws fought in a ring, facing outward. Os had trouble picking out the camouflaged sand striders until one leapt through the air against the blue of the sky. The Snapjaw raised a hide buckler just in time to block the fangs, but the eight legs scrabbled at the edges with savage strength until a brief opening emerged. Flinging the shield aside, the Snapjaw whirled and drove its spear into the spider's back, pinning it to the sand. Other arachnids exploited the opening in the circle just as Sward arrived howling.

The battle cry startled the sand striders, some leaping in the air and spinning to face the new threat. Snapjaw spears stabbed and axes crunched into the distracted spiders. The orderly canid ring broke as their savagery took control. Fangs and claws ripped legs and raked eyes. Growls, yelps, and howls rose into the sky as circling shadows hailed the arrival of airborne opportunists. Os jabbed with his spear, slammed his shield into a hairy leg, and heard it crunch. He skewered a leaping sand strider, its weight ripping the spear from his grasp. Snapping out fist and heels, he clubbed another and watched it curl its legs in death.

A yip sent him diving away and rolling to his feet. Sward stood over the hairy body of a strider that had snuck up behind Os, now a wreck of broken legs and leaking abdomen. He spun back into the fray as Os recovered his spear. Amid the swirling sand and chaos, Os saw furred bodies motionless on the ground, some already bloated by poisoned bites. Crumpled spiders lay among the bodies, but a few sand striders cartwheeled away from the scene of carnage.

Os wiped futilely at the sand stuck to his sweaty brow, blinked dust out of his eyes, and panted. Sward backed toward him, eyes on two slowly advancing Snapjaws. Sward answered their growls with a snarl of his own. Os' heart jumped in his chest. He rose on the balls of his feet and lowered the spear at the beings they had just saved from death.

"What did you expect?" Os projected into Sward's mind.

"He," Sward jabbed to the left Snapjaw, "is the lone surviving male. She," he pointed to the other, "is in heat. That's why we're here."

Os realized then that Sward didn't fully expect to survive their quest for the Hzeens. He wished to sew his seed in this Snapjaw female. A typical Spire dweller produced few seeds in a lifetime, perhaps a dozen if truly blessed. Sward would likely have few chances to sire an heir before they reached the Boiling Rift. Os would have none, too young to produce a seed or find a mate.

The growling continued, punctuated by yips and the clapping of jaws. Slowly the male advanced past the female toward Sward. Os took the cue and held back behind his friend. The rivals began circling each other, and Os realized he would have to fight both Snapjaws if Sward fell. After several tense moments, the male tucked his tail and bolted away, still within sight but completely cowed. Os watched with curiosity as the female presented. Sward held out his left hand, and the spine shot into her flank. With a whine, she scurried off in the direction of the intimidated male.

Sward looked rather pleased with himself, Os thought. Swooping shapes caught his attention, black wings descending to feast. Sward paid them no mind, cleaning the head of his spear in the sand and taking off at a run. A few hours of light remained, and Os doubted there would be another break.

*   *   *

Sward shook Os awake and drank from his skin. He had dug a hole at the base of some rocks and found a bit of water, but they would need more before they reached the Hzeen.

"Yes. I have a place in mind," Sward answered his concern. "A spring remembered from my last visit to the Rift."

"Surely it's guarded. Something that precious in the Waste is always claimed by someone."

"Who else dares the Boiling Rift save the Spire dwellers? Who assembles to meet the Rift's threat when the cycle is at hand? It's not time for the Riftspawn to overflow into the Waste and consume everything in reach, but others fear it just the same. It will be unguarded." He resigned to Sward's confidence with another swallow of murky water.

Os watched first as Sward slept, and Sward's turn was uneventful aside from a couple of rattlers that sought out the warmth of Os' prone body. He offered one decapitated snake to Os. They quickly stripped the flesh from the bones and washed it down with a few sips of water. The two jogged while they waited for the warmth of the sun to invigorate them. Os knew Sward would set a quick pace after that.

"Will the seed grow?" Os knew little of this, only that it was not his own time. It was not part of Mangijin's teachings.

"It is rare for the seed to fail, rare for the pup not to grow strong if the mother is hardy. More common for the pup to die on its way to the Spire once it comes of age, but even that is rare." He wondered if it were true and smiled at the thought of Sward's pup.

"You are not old. Why not wait until after you hold your Hzeen to make a better choice of a mate?" Os adjusted his shield more tightly, preparing for the increased pace.

"You question my choice of mate?" Sward spun on Os, spear tilted slightly toward the boy.

"No. I only remember your claim that the tribes further into the Waste are stronger, better warriors." Os' eyes never left the point of the spear. "Like the one your mother was from."

Sward's answer was to run. Os cursed himself. He should have known better than to question Sward. The canid made a decision and would always defend it as the right one, even if he didn't reveal all of his reasons. He scrambled to catch up to his friend as Sward's shadow faintly fled before him.

Several hours later, Sward slowed. Os gratefully joined him minutes later, unstopping his water skin and slinging his shield. Os had expected a pool, perhaps even marked by a stone wall, but the spring failed to impress. Sward lay on his stomach, long tongue lapping a puddle. When he finished, he filled his skin and gestured for Os to do the same. The water felt blessedly cool, but filling the skin seemed to take ages. Despite the delay, they offered thanks to Chorpaneshi.

The Boiling Rift lay just beyond a hill of small rocks that made for treacherous footing. The Riftborn discarded rock at the rift's edge. Over time, the stones formed a slope and tumbled down to the plain below. Os dismissed the possibility of finding Sward's Hzeen somewhere in the rocky detritus. He felt Sward would have claimed it by now if that were the case. His friend proceeded cautiously up the side of the hill, occasionally sending a small slide of pebbles for Os to dodge.

Sward fell to all fours near the summit, waving his muzzle back and forth. Os joined him on his right, falling flat to limit his profile against the sky. The Rift fell away below them. The walls were nearly vertical, ending at a narrow floor perhaps 50 strides distant. Near the floor, they were pocked here and there with dark openings. Os was prepared for scuttling activity, but nothing moved below.

Sward planted his spear shaft within the rocks at the summit, and Os did the same. The canid played out the rope of braided root fibers and tied the end to the anchoring spears. With his shield slung over his back, he descended in careful slides, occasionally using a foot to rest against the wall. Os waited until Sward reached the floor and began his own descent. He wanted to rush from his vulnerable position, but he dared not risk burning his hands or losing his grip.

Os relied on Sward's senses to guide them to one of the many similar openings. While Sward was armed with teeth and claws, Os had only a single knife and his shield. Neither comforted him much as they entered the darkness. The knife was constructed from a Riftborn's mandible, and Os suddenly worried it might be bad luck given their current surroundings.

Sward's eyes needed little adjustment to the darkness. Thankfully, he paused to allow Os's eyes more time. Here and there, flecks of luminescent fungi grew in acrid slime along the walls as they did in the Spire, but they provided too little light for quick travel. Os sparingly dispensed the oils from the Spire fungi onto the hide-wrapped handle of his knife and held it by the back of the blade like a torch. Sometimes the pitch of the tunnel fluctuated wildly, causing them to slide noisily in the loose gravel, so he sheathed his knife in favor of a steadying hand. Os imagined they slowly descended, but Sward would not or could not tell him for certain.

The canid stopped so abruptly that Os nearly ran into him. In the weak glow from his knife handle, he saw Sward gazing downward from the termination of the tunnel. The smell of Riftborn droppings made his nostrils tingle.

"The floor of a cavern rests six strides below. My Hzeen is close. My father's call fills my head." Sward leapt into darkness, a muffled crunch signaling his landing. Os followed, rolling to his feet a short distance from his friend.

The stench of the droppings threatened to gag Os, and he wondered how Sward could possibly tolerate it. Breathing through his nose nauseated him, but he knew it would be worse if he opened his mouth. Mounds of waste were piled throughout the large chamber. Riftborn drones little larger than Os' shield skittered among the piles. They scattered before Sward until he covered the diameter of the cavern and entered an opening unlike the others. This one looked to Os like a fissure that narrowed to a close a span above his head. "The Riftborn use their feces to plug gaps and shore up the walls and ceilings." Sward tapped the tunnel wall. "They have to digest it first, foul creatures."

"Will the small ones bring soldiers?"

"Of course, but they are few this time of year. Not until the next cycle will there be a true army of them." Os managed to suppress his telepathic link to Sward before his companion could pick up on his fear. It might only take one of the giants to kill them if they were caught in a tunnel.

Down they climbed, this time at a more regular descent that deviated from the fissure and made for better footing. Os applied more fungal oils to his knife handle. The light trembled to match his hand, and he tried to convince himself it was growing cold as their path took them deeper. The caverns beneath the Spire chilled him the same both with cold and potential dangers, but he tried not to dwell on his home. It was far away, and he was unwelcome until their tests were completed.

"Huxley's seed!" Sward's blaspheme hit Os like a slap in the face, but he understood his friend's alarm. Before them, in another large chamber, rose a central pillar so thick that Sward and Os could not circle it with their clasped arms. Thin cross beams ringed it at irregular intervals and connected it to the walls, swathed in fungal light at each junction. The canid ran to it and then around it, disappearing from view. Os followed him to find Sward scratching at the pillar. When digging with his nails proved futile, Sward growled and pounded the pillar with his fists. His frustrated growling gave way to shrill whining. The Riftborn had encased Sward's Hzeen, and likely what remained of the canid's hand, in their solidified filth.

"Sward, stop," Os begged. He searched in vain for a stone large enough to hammer the pillar. The next sound stopped him cold.

Sward pounded the edge of his shield against the stubborn surface. Tiny chips flew away under the onslaught but obviously disappointed the canid. Os imagined the roof caving in on them with every chunking blow and following scrape of the shield. Would such proximity of his own Hzeen drive him to such madness? He could only wonder with dread.

"Help me." The canid puffed in his exertions. His voice in Os' head belied his crazed determination and a vision of the pulsing, green Hzeen cemented into the pillar. So far, no opposition rushed them, but how long could such fortune last? A thin crack formed. A long shard broke free and shattered against the floor. Os needed no further prompting.

The two alternated their blows against the pillar. Between their turns, Os scanned for enemies near the openings in the sides of the chamber. Periodically, Sward pulled at the marred surface, only managing to dislodge tiny fragments. The carapace dropped between them like a bolder, but Sward's reflexes saved him. He spun away, bringing his shield to bear.

The meager light shone off the Riftborn's prodigious bulk while its pointed legs scraped grooves into the earthen floor. Os took a deep breath and clamped down doors around his psyche, shutting out the sound and stemming his fear. He heaved at the side of the sturdy exoskeleton, attempting to tip their foe and expose the joints of legs and thorax. Mangajin's iron grip was more easily bested. In desperation, Os stabbed clumsily under the carapace with his knife. It caught and rewarded him with a sticky flow of ichor down his forearm, but the weapon lodged and slipped from his hand.

The creature spun awkwardly in response to the wound but showed no signs of pain. Os leapt backward and barely avoided its scything mandibles.

From behind it, Sward grabbed one of its legs and tugged the creature away from Os. It tried to spin back toward Sward and wrenched its leg at a rending angle. Sward followed with a blow from the edge of his shield that severed the leg at its lower joint. Os lowered a shoulder and drove into its side, trying once more to tip the creature. Sward spun away to add his strength to Os's, and together they unbalanced their foe.

A flailing insectoid leg scraped a gash across Os's forehead as the two heaved their enemy over onto its back. Os ripped at a leg while Sward chopped with his shield. Os recovered his knife and dug into the tender seams in the underbelly. Slowly the blows took a toll on the Riftborn until it twitched and lay still.

Os dabbed at his bleeding forehead with the palm of his hand and winced. The gash throbbed hotly as his muscles began to quake. The Riftborn's fluids already crusted over the skin of his knuckles. The closeness of their deaths weighed on his shoulders. Never had he seen a Riftborn so large.

"My Hzeen must be free." Sward turned back to the column, and hammered it with the edge of his shield. "How can you not feel it?" With a thought, Sward pushed his own perceptions briefly into Os's mind. The song of Sward's Hzeen thrummed down into his belly. It pulled at him, so close but still encased in the Riftborn cement.

"We should come back with tools," Os began. "We could not have known it would be trapped inside the rock." He impotently flicked the ichor from his hand then tried to scrape it against the rim of his shield. Sward gazed upward at the beams. When Os lifted his head, his heart stopped.

Three Riftborn the size of their fallen enemy climbed across beams above them. Os thought he saw movement further up the column when he dove away from the first falling assailant. A second fell between Sward and Os, blocking the canid's retreat with its bulk. The third landed behind him and snapped Sward's head from his shoulders in one vicious clack of its jaws.

Os ran.

Tears streamed down Os' face at his own cowardice, but his legs still drove him onward. The tunnel left little room to fight, even if bravery overwhelmed his good sense. He scrabbled on all fours when the passage steepened and paused briefly to judge his pursuers' distance. Years of exploring the Spire's caverns and wormholes had made him instinctively ingrain his path in memory, but his fear screamed at him only to run. He fought to slow his breathing, focus his thoughts, and find his way.

The scraping behind him grew louder, and the tunnel seemed to narrow around him. He took a drink, wholly inadequate to slake his thirst, and pushed on through the darkness. The sound of his labored breathing changed subtly as he neared the entrance into the first cavern he and Sward had entered together. He spilled into it by himself, but not alone.

Two large Riftborn guarded his escape. Though smaller than those he and Sward had fought below, dread passed through Os to set his guts quaking and heart pounding. He muttered a brief prayer and swerved for one of the side passages.

Only one of his enemies followed in earnest. Os slowed to let it advance on him as far as possible. With a last burst of speed, he jumped over its head before it could rise. He landed on its back as it started to spin, the motion turning his second leap into a fall. Twisting himself in the air, he rolled across his shield and onto his feet to begin a new sprint for the exit.

The second giant beetle stood firmly planted in front of his intended route, head lowered, mandibles already parted to rip flesh. He swung his shield in from the side, heard the mandible snap where it protruded from the head. The wounded Riftborn reflexively spun. Fearing the enemy behind him, Os vaulted the enraged beetle in front of him and darted into the passage.

He plunged out into the ravine where the number of small Riftborn threatened to overwhelm him. Smashing with his shield and feet, he cleared a path. Though the small enemies had fled him earlier, their courage seemed bolstered by their substantial numbers. He hurled between groups of Riftborn as they threatened to congeal into a solid mass of death.

He spotted the rope blowing in the breeze and prayed to Chorpaneshi for the strength to climb. Sheathing his knife and slinging his shield across his back, he jumped and grabbed the rope as far from the ravine's floor as possible. He fought briefly to clamp the rope between his feet. The Riftborn were likely scaling the side with their sharp feet, but he dared not look down. His fear led to shame, his shame to anger, and his anger to strength. He needed to live, even if only to mourn his friend.

At last, he scrambled over the edge. The spears had bent but not broken or come loose from the rocks. Now he strained to pull them free as the first of the Riftborn appeared. He settled for a rock as large as his head and catapulted it with both hands. It smashed one of the Riftborn's legs but hardly slowed the beast.

He freed his spear and cracked the carapace hard enough to flip it over the edge of the ravine. As another Riftborn climbed into view, he buried the spear's point in its small head, thin black blood gushing forth as he ripped it free. Abandoning Sward's spear and the rope, he hopped through the rock field as quickly as he could. A few of the smallest Riftborn took flight to harass him. He bludgeoned them away with the butt of his spear, sending them careening into the rocks below. Turning to face another, he shrank back as it exploded a stride in front of him.

The thunderous roar filled the expanse, and he turned to see a small army before him. Smoke puffed away from one of the mutants who bore what Os only assumed was the projectile thrower that had killed the Riftborn. Two more weapons like it were pointed at Os. He looked behind him to see the beetles abandon their pursuit.

"Get down here," growled a huge mutant even larger than Sward had been. He wore a shining, scaled vest that matched the caps on twin tusks growing from his jaws. Os merely had to look at the string of captives chained together to know his fate. His fighting odds were slim. If he ran, the mutants mounted on the fleet-footed Terror Birds would bring him down. He descended slowly to give himself time to think, but no plan materialized by the time he was commanded to drop his shield and weapons.

Two well-armed mutants approached him after his spear hit the dirt. They snapped a collar around his neck and manacles around his wrists, laughing as they fought over his water. Before Os realized what was happening, he wrapped the smaller mutant's neck in his manacles and snapped his neck. Others rushed forward, and Os fell under a rain of savage blows. When they tired of kicking him, they dragged him to the back of a column of dirt-encrusted humans. Some were wounded, and all looked exhausted. The captors tied him to the end of the line while others finished drinking at the spring. The large mutant screamed something Os could not understand, and the column of slaves shuffled forward.

A few minutes later, the man in front of Os looked back at him over his shoulder with a grin. Os did not feel inclined to make friends at the moment and only nodded.

"That was extremely stupid, my friend. Benchley," the man said in the trade tongue most used by humans. Os had no idea what the last word meant until the captive asked his question. "What's your name?"

The sentence took Os a moment to understand, still thinking in the dialect of the Spire.

"Os." Pronouncing the name deep in his throat made his pummeled jaws ache. He longed to use the Silent Speech with this man and possibly learn their destination, but humans seldom had the gift of the Spire dwellers. Before more could be said, a mutant covered with boils cuffed Os on the back of his head to restore silence. It sent him a message about how he should behave for the next few days' march.

Failure and grief dragged at him. With neither Hzeen in his possession, Os' promises to the Elders echoed in his mind. Ravnid's confidence in him exacerbated the churning in his gut, and he could never forgive himself for Sward's death. He wondered how many of these prisoners might have plotted escape but still remained in chains. These men were once strong, but they could not be measured against one blessed by Chorpaneshi. They were like Huxley had been when he first arrived at the Spire. Os would be no mutant's slave, even if it meant his death, and he was eager to see if Benchley felt the same.

Os only broke the rule of silence once to laugh nearly uncontrollably, and he paid with the sole thing he could: the currency of pain. It mattered little to him, as long as they didn't kill him. He found himself looking forward to each day's progress despite the scant food, exhausting passage, and brutal treatment. Its call to him grew stronger every day. Each step in the march led him closer to his father's killers, to his vengeance, and to his Hzeen. Ω

Introducing the
Fantastical Fiction Feature
on NonlocalSciFi.com

100% FREE short stories that you can read any time on
NonlocalSciFi.com.

"What's In A Name?"
by Nicholas C. Rossis

"Dumped From Spinning Ship"
by John Grey

"Perspectives"
by David Reinersmann

Plus many more! Only on NonlocalSciFi.com.

Jumpers

Written By
Victor G. Espinosa

"Gentlemen, we have ten minutes 'til jump."

A boisterous shout consisting of whoops, yells, and screams went up from the commandos strapped to their seats. Ten minutes was the mark to check your equipment one last time in preparation for the jump. Commandos continued to shout and yell as their seats unstrapped themselves and lowered into the deck seamlessly.

Screaming and beating their armor, helmets, and each other, the ESS, or Elite Strike Squad, on the third deck of the S.G.U. Warhawk did whatever was necessary to get their blood and adrenaline pumping, not that it wasn't already flowing in excess amounts. Being a paid warrior and having more excitement in one night than most people have in their whole lives is what attracted them to this line of work. The unique mind of a Jumper was something that no psychologist could yet accurately describe. So far, the most common word used in group studies was "impaired."

Amidst the shouting and yelling, there were a few warriors that used silence and meditation to quicken their minds before a jump. One such man was Keith Karr.

Keith stood off to the aft of the ship with all his equipment double-checked and green-lighted, looking over a map of the assault ground on his HUD. His armor was distinct in that it wasn't a perfect model like most others suits. He had gauntlets over five years old but had a breastplate more advanced than any other on the ship, made specifically for this jump. His helmet was a relic that he had grown more accustomed to than his own face, and the life support data was located on his shoulder and forearm instead of his back. His armor was accented with deep blue lines running from his helmet, down the front of his torso and legs, and ending at the tops of his boots.

At a glance, any one could tell Keith Karr was different from the rest of the commandos gearing up for the jump. More than his armor and demeanor separated him from the crowd; he had a mission here more important than fulfilling a psychotic lust for violence.

"Gentlemen, five minutes to jump."

Another shout went up from the third deck of the S.G.U. Warhawk and continued until a live feed broke into everyone's HUD. The commotion died and everyone quieted to watch.

Keith minimized the satellite view of their jump ground and focused on the feed. A man with dark gray hair and round cheeks sat in a large, black chair resting his hands on a table made of black plaster. Behind him, the dark expanse of space swallowed his figure and outlined him with stars. His face was serious, but his eyes held desperation and need. Keith noted the man wasn't formally dressed; just a shirt and tie, no jacket.

"Men of the 104th ESS. God, I love you, Jumpers." said the Head of Colony, Brian Grondus.

A shout unlike the ones before it shook the innards of the Warhawk as it rocketed toward its destination, the men reveling in a compliment by the highest political figure they knew.

"Today is a terrible day for our planet. After having our consulates on the Republic of Dratis bombed and tarred, we have had reports that several of our diplomats and representatives have been kidnapped and are being held hostage by the rebel force on Dratis." The Head of Colony paused, and his face grew more harrowing with a blink. "But today is also a terrible day for the people who inhabit planet Drati. Today is the day when we remind them who supports whom and just who is in charge. After weeks of struggle with these rebels, I will not have Tetran look foolish and weak in the face of this attack! Place a foothold, soldiers, and let's take back this planet!"

The men of the Warhawk shouted for glory and rage across all decks and frequencies. Keith muted his helmet audio receptors and still felt the vibrations through his boots and rattling his clips.

"Gentlemen, two minutes to jump. Fly fast, hawks."

Keith felt slight maneuvering as the ship began to dip into the high atmosphere around Datri. He didn't feel any evasive flying, so at least the ground forces weren't firing yet. Keith checked his shoulder and remembered that his insignia marked him as colonel after his previous mission, which meant most of the Jumpers would be looking to him for direction. He did a quick glance around the hold, assisted by his HUD, to see that most of the Jumpers were lieutenants and privates. He wasn't completely alone, but he definitely didn't have company high up the ranks.

As the commandos started lining up at the mag-hatch in the aft of the ship, most gave a quick nod to Keith to show they recognized him and his command. He nodded in turn to most but didn't bother after a while. He wouldn't be seeing much of them after the jump.

His HUD crackled with a sudden connection and Head of Colony Brian

Grondus appeared again, this time with a much more measured look on his face and the beautiful, star spotted expanse behind him littered with ships lighting their engines and drifting away.

"Keith." A pause as he took in breath. "I can't tell you how important this is to us. If she…if they find out she's on planet, they'll not just kill her. They will rip her to shreds on live feed to the whole galaxy. Keith, if that happens I don't think I would be able to take it. My soul would just…I couldn't live with—"

"Head of Colony Grondus, I am fully aware of what's at stake here. I know the mission."

Grondus looked into the feed that translated straight to Keith's eyes. "You come back too, Keith. This war is only starting, and you are the only person I can rely on for this."

"Understood, Head of Colony. I'm jumping now."

Grondus nodded once, his eyes boring into Keith's memory forever, and the feed died.

"What'cha looking at, grandpa?" A voice chimed in over Keith's helmet com.

He looked past the dead feed to notice a young commando eyeing him with one hand on his hip and the other on his gun. Keith noticed that the gun in question was a customized R-88 Kec Rifle with the commando's finger resting firmly on the trigger. Keith looked at the boy through his opaque helmet.

"Finger off the trigger," he said. "Unless you want to shoot one of us."

The young soldier looked abashed for a moment before adopting a more professional stance with his weapon. Keith noticed that he had himself a group of followers who'd been attracted to his colonel insignia and were waiting for his orders. He fell into the habit of command.

"Line up for the jump," he yelled. "One at a time. One second interval in between. Keep armor live but weapons cold until given the signal. At fifteen hundred feet, activate the casing on your armor and make sure your lives are green."

Some Jumpers were nodding their heads at his commands, others were checking their equipment, while some looked like they were just itching to get out and kill something. Keith moved back towards the mag-field while yelling orders. "Once on the ground, find your platoon and move to your A.O. Each team knows their color and designated C.A. Don't mess this up."

"Let's kill some Dratis!" someone screamed from the back, and others replied in earnest.

Keith turned around to face the aft mag-hatch just in time to see the proiron protection slide back and the blue field power to life, bathing the entire deck in a soft glow. Darkness punctuated by random clouds dominated the view outside the hatch until a large streak of green energy blasted its way spaceward, barely missing the aft burners of the Warhawk.

Keith grabbed the nearest support handle and yelled to the men behind him, "Hold on!" a second before the pilot yelled over their helmet coms, "Evasive maneuvers, ground fire! Jump! Jump! Jump!"

More blasts of green whizzed by the Warhawk as it dipped and dived and slewed side to side in the sky. During one of its maneuvers, Keith spotted their escort ships doing their best to dodge the incoming fire as well. The lights on the deck of the Warhawk began signaling them for jump, flashing different colors in consecutive order for each platoon. Keith let go of his support and made for the mag-field just as the young commando from earlier rushed passed him and leaped out into the atmosphere.

"Time to fly, grandpa!" he screamed before disappearing.

"Idiot," Keith muttered, then launched himself from the Warhawk with a running start.

The familiar sensation of a jump flooded his body with all the adrenaline and euphoria that he had been missing these last few years. Though it was perfect silence encased in his airtight armor, Keith could hear his blood pumping louder than ever as he plummeted to the planet's surface. The momentary beauty of high atmosphere cloud vistas with the perfect amount of star and moonlight was lost in the face of crisscrossing beams rising from the planet surface. Energy pulses the size of the personnel craft shot up at the Jumpers and their transports in an attempt to blast them out of the sky

Keith tried not to smile as the old sensation of fearlessness cascaded across his nervous system. He knew that most other commandos augmented themselves with chemicals, amps, or implants, but this feeling was all natural for Keith. It's what had made him chose to be a Jumper for fourteen years. But after retiring and spending so long simply existing on the surface of a planet, he had almost forgotten what it was like to soar down to one.

Black blurs accompanied Keith during the descent; other Jumpers falling at varying speeds, trying to avoid clustering against the ground fire. Keith noticed a Jumper disappear in a wave of green and turn immediately to vapor. It was a fate that he wished to avoid, so he turned his attention downward once again. Though it was impossible to see where the fire was coming from since they were still above the clouds, the Jumpers spun, twisted, and controlled their descents in order to stay alive.

A loud crack sounded over Keith's helmet com, and he felt the air vibrate behind him. He strained his neck to turn just in time to see pieces of the S.G.U. Warhawk explode in fiery shrapnel, one of the ground cannons scoring a direct hit. Keith faced the clouds he was rapidly approaching and hoped his mission wouldn't end before it even had time to begin.

He passed into the upper layer of vaporous dust particles that had looked solid only moments before. As Keith passed through them at high speeds, it felt like a shower of dirty water. In seconds, he had passed the clouds and saw what the inhabitants of Dratis had set up as defense. It was night on the planet, and their drop zone target was a forest next to the city of Bar'sha. He did a quick sweep of the city as he approached and saw that all the machinery was anti-craft guns aimed spaceward with little in the way of actual ground forces. If his fellow Jumpers survived the descent, this would be almost too easy.

Keith's HUD flashed a proximity warning, and he activated his suit's concrete ability. He felt his joints stiffen and his chest received extra pressure as his armor compacted and solidified in preparation for landing. A proiron shield slid over his faceplate, but Keith closed his eyes anyways and counted down in perfect sync with the timer on his HUD. His armor crashed into soft earth and buried twelve feet deep in dirt and grass and mud. The HUD stayed green and ran checks to ensure all systems were functional. Slowly, the pressure around Keith's chest lessened. Soon he'd have control of his body again.

This was, however, the scariest part for many Jumpers, when they were at their most vulnerable. It was not often, but if an enemy had advance warning of a jump or was able to get to the drop zone right as the Jumpers were landing, they were rewarded with a brief opportunity to kill the semi-invincible soldiers without a fight. A quick shotgun to the faceplate while a soldier was waiting for control of their armor was a dark thing to crawl out of the ground and witness. Keith had seen it happen several times, lucky he was not the victim, and now as he lay waiting for his joints to open again, it was all he could think about. Time seemed to drag as he counted and focused on his breathing.

His HUD beeped, and active coms came online the same moment that his armor released. Keith rose from the hole he had created, activated his kinetic barriers, and drew his Grog Rifle while staying low to the ground. Jumpers were crashing at intervals around him, and some had already begun advancing on the enemy position. Keith stayed in a hunched position and closed the ground to the nearest firing platform.

Healthy green grass turned abruptly to steel as he walked in order to support the massive firing platform that housed over a dozen different munitions options for skyward attacks. Jumpers were advance units usually sent in to destroy such outposts, paving the way for the main force to come in a crush the enemy. Normally, Keith loved the tactics and strategy involved, and that is what had gotten him his job in an office instead of on the ground. But this night on Dratis was different. He wasn't operating with the unit of Jumpers.

Keith waited just past the guard-railing for the firing platform and hunched behind crates of ammunition. Several soldiers made their way up the same path and past him to take out the guns. Keith nodded to all of them and gave several hand signals to ensure they spread out evenly and focused on the key areas. When most had passed and were occupied with their own duties, Keith ducked back into the woods where he had just crashed and made his way east.

He had studied the map of his objective a hundred times, almost to the point of memorization, as he marked the rooms and buildings. Yet he still drew up the map on his HUD and eyed the path to the Bright Learners School of Bar'sha just to be sure. After looking at his route options again, he started off on a different approach angle to the city that would take him around the firing platform, all the while pondering why the people of Drati would use a school for a makeshift prison.

He had less than a hundred meters of brush and cover to get through before he could enter the city, coming out of the forest right behind the school. He stayed crouched the whole way and had plenty of time to reflect on how long it had been since his last jump or any mission at all. His muscles were burning but loving the exercise, and his mind hadn't been this clear in ages. His blood was raging through his body, and he only wished he could listen to some historic rock through his helmet as he went.

Far to Keith's right, bushes and trees moved about unnaturally, and he stopped immediately. Hoping that whatever was moving hadn't seen him, he stayed perfectly still.

"Human! The signal is red!" A garbled voice shouted from the distance.

Keith cursed as gunfire ricocheted off his kinetic barrier and more splattered the dirt around him. He took a diving roll and came up on his knees with the image from his rifle scope feeding through to his HUD, eliminating the need to aim down the sights. From the hip, Keith fired three times and watched on heightened sensors as three heads imploded. The bodies looked almost human without their elongated heads and long snouts as they fell to the ground.

Keith double-timed it through the rest of the woods, staying low but not bothering to crouch on the ground. He burst from the cover of foliage at a full sprint and watched his HUD track his signal on the map of Bar'sha city. The school was right in front of him with its lights on, but there was a fiber fence that he had to get through first. The razor-sharp barrier looked deadly enough, sitting benignly in the pale light of Drati's two half-moons. Keith had seen one activate once and knew just how quickly a man could die on it.

Keeping his full speed momentum, Keith used the augmentation of his armor to give him an extra boost as he jumped clear over the two meter fence. He landed on the other side in a roll and came up aiming with his HUD and a finger on the trigger, ready to fire.

No alarm went off, and no one came running outside. The school stayed silent for now. Keith got to his feet and dashed to a back door that had cover. He checked his surroundings and then peeked through the long window in the door.

The hallway inside was brightly lit. Pale green laminate covered every surface, from the floor to the ceilings. Keith used his helmet to zoom down the hallway and noticed shadows moving behind a door. Once again, he brought up the map of the school and saw the quickest path from his doorway to where her red X was. Then he reminded himself that this was a rescue mission, not a kill-order. The Primarch came first; he didn't need to kill everyone on site beforehand, he only needed to ensure her safety. This wasn't like the old days, and he had to make sure he remembered that.

With more power from his armor routed through his gauntlets, Keith knocked the locking mechanism off the door and proceeded inside as quietly as possible. He crouched down again and felt the familiar burn in his leg muscles as he made his way down the corridor. He paused in a small alcove for a drinking fountain, effectively covered on three sides, and decided to check up on the battle with the rest of the Jumpers before going any further. He opened his coms to active commandos and pulled up a few visual feeds from them as well.

The sight brought back memories as, from a first person point of view, Keith watched solider after soldier plow ahead in battle, letting bullets and projectiles of all sorts bounce off their shields and armor. The alien races of the Republic of Dratis died at the feet of soldiers far too advanced for them to repel.

"Go go go go!"

"Drop the charge, man! Woo!"

"I'm gonna kill 'em all!"

"Fire! Fire!"

"Come on, killers! Where's grandpa at?!"

Keith turned off the coms, satisfied that the Jumpers were creating the distraction he needed. They were almost too good; they might make it to the school before Keith had time to escape. He dropped the visual feeds and gripped his rifle in advance position.

Coming around the corner of the alcove he was hiding in, the hallway hadn't changed. He made his way to the stairs leading to the school's basement at the end of the hallway, his eyes constantly flashing between the hallway he walked and the scope of his rifle in case targets appeared. Three did.

Coming from the stairs Keith was hoping to reach, three large Yarkos came lumbering up it with proiron cudgels in their hands. Yarkos' weren't the smartest race on Drati, Keith recalled from the briefing, but based on their physiology, they were probably the hardest to kill. They stood over two meters at the least, and preferred to beat their enemies to death before eating most of their flesh. Keith's mind worked through all of this once he saw the hulking, yellowish bodies emerge from the stairwell.

The first Yarkos spotted him immediately, and Keith opened fire with secondary and primary munitions on his rifle. Both muzzles flashed bright as two different types of ammo punctured the Yarkos through. It didn't have time to scream as it fell to the floor, smoking and dead.

The second and third Yarkos launched themselves at Keith with weapons held high. Keith waited and then dodged the first Yarkos' club at the last second. Using his momentum, he slipped inside the third Yarkos' guard and activated his silencer. Two long, extremely sharp blades of proiron extended from Keith's left gauntlet and electrified. He plunged them as far as he could into the Yarkos' side before it could swing at him, and the alien howled. Its body convulsed and shook, Keith's arm still embedded in it. Before the remaining Yarkos could raise his club for another attack, Keith held down the trigger and fired the last of his clip into its throat and watched the creature fall to the ground dead.

The sounds he and his adversaries made were sure to attract attention, Keith reasoned, quickly reloading his rifle and placing it into the halo on his back. He dashed down the hall and to the stairs while drawing and switching his heavy pistol to incendiary rounds. No use wasting rifle ammo in close quarters.

Once in the basement area of the school, Keith could see why they'd chosen the school for a prison. The "classrooms" were fortified better than most military prisons Keith had seen, and everything was old fashioned steel. The long hallway before him was dark with hanging lights every few meters casting a cone of bright white on the floor. Doors stood to either side along the corridor, but only a few had the glow of a light from within.

Keith walked slowly and stayed focused on the red 'X' on his HUD. Her red 'X'. It was all that mattered. He had made it this far, which meant that there was still hope he'd be able to get her out before any reinforcements arrived.

Keith stopped outside of a door several inches thick with a faint light showing through the crack on the floor. He looked at the hinges of the door and the locking mechanism, trying to figure out the quickest and quietest way through. He decided on the overload route and extended his silencer again. He stabbed it into the key recognition and flooded the door with reverse currents. It popped open slightly, but he still had to put his weight into it for it to swing open.

Inside, a woman was dangling with her feet barely scraping the ground from a metal pipe in the ceiling, bound by plastic rope around her wrists. She was looking down at the floor, but Keith could see blood and bruises on her face. He holstered his pistol and ran up to her to cut the bonds that held her. She collapsed in his arms and whimpered from the pain. He covered her mouth, and her eyes flashed open, confused and in pain. After a moment, they found his, looking through his faceplate, and slowly she began to realize.

"I'm sorry I cut you down so quickly. Your arms are going to hurt as blood gets back to them." He took his hand away from her mouth. "I didn't have time to be gentle. We really need to go."

Her face looked tired. She blinked rapidly as he spoke, but he wasn't sure she was fully understanding his words. She opened her mouth to speak, but Keith heard a sound from behind. His HUD confirmed his suspicions.

"Hold that thought," he said.

He turned and dashed out of the Primarch's cell just as an alien came around it ready to fire. Keith slammed into it with augmented force and drove it against the adjacent wall. He activated his silencer again and moved the gut the creature but saw his weapon shatter against its black armor instead. Keith looked up into the faceplate of a very angry Tyrin commando and realized reinforcements had gotten here more quickly than expected.

The Tyrin swung an elbow at him, but Keith ducked and pushed himself away from his enemy. He drew his pistol again and fired as fast as his finger twitched. The flame rounds overloaded the Tyrin's shields quickly, and the rest of the clip emptied into its gut. He turned the way he had entered the hallway to see several more commandos coming down the stairs. He pulled out his Grog rifle again and changed his secondary fire to grenades, firing three of them down the hallway. He grabbed a remote ripper grenade from his halo and dropped it next to the alien's body.

Walking back inside the Primarch's cell and making sure each grenade's detonator was designated on his gauntlets powerpanel, Keith prepared himself for one hell of a fight. Primarch Shiren was standing now but hunched over and still not looking wholly healthy. Keith walked over to her and offered his shoulder.

"We don't have much time," he said while reaching around her right ear and deactivating the holoface she was wearing. "I can't believe this lasted the whole time," he whispered in awe as a face he had never seen before dematerialized and Primarch Shiren's real face appeared. "If they had scanned you for devices and found out who you really were…" He trailed off.

"They just beat me the old fashioned way," she said. "They never suspected someone so important would be here now. It was a mistake for me to come, obviously, I see that now. But the council was so convinced, and the colony needed…Well, never mind that now." Shiren was panting, her face still had blood on it, and she looked exhausted.

"Like I was saying, we don't have much time," Keith said. "Can you run?"

"No."

"Then you know what that means. Hang on tight. This is going to get close." He touched a button on his gauntlet, and the hallway behind him filled with acrid smoke.

"Give me a gun," Shiren said groggily.

"Are you drugged? No way." Keith hoisted the Primarch on his shoulder and touched the second button on his gauntlet, setting off a high-pitched explosion outside. Keith dashed out the door and past three commandos who had been ripped to shreds by motorized razor spheres courtesy of his grenade and then shot a fourth commando point blank in the faceplate with his rifle's concentrated fire. The acrid smoke was harmless to humans, but it had been engineered to be deadly to virtually any other species. The ripper he had set off ricocheted tiny blades down every inch of the hallway. Keith used it as an opportunity to headshot several more Tyrins as they tried to get their bearings and probably wondered why they were bleeding through their armor.

Keith ran through the hallway and up the stairs, leaving a small unit of commandos dead in his wake.

"Give me a gun," Shiren said again.

"Shut up!" Keith yelled while running down the bright, laminated hallway. His HUD alerted him to more targets approaching from the left at a hallway intersection. When Keith sprinted past it, he didn't even bother to turn his head to fire. He just kept running towards the door he'd broken in through just moments ago.

"Give me a gun."

"No."

Shiren squirmed on his shoulder for a moment, and then Keith heard gunfire behind him just as he reached the exit. He turned to see two more dead bodies on the floor with smoking holes in their torsos. He glanced up at Shiren to see her holding his heavy pistol.

"Why'd you stop running?" she asked.

Keith kicked the door open and dashed outside of the school into the night and headed to the extraction point. He could hear gunfire all around them, and dense smoke rose from the direction of the gun platform. Keith pulled up Bar'sha's map while skirting the side of the school and entered the main roads of the city. He had seven blocks to go before turning west and then it was a straight run to the pick-up. It wasn't a long run, but Keith was tired already from shouldering the Primarch.

Two large gunships with forward lights shining swooped overhead and through the city streets, weaving between buildings, as they made their way south. Keith continued running and prepared himself for what he'd do if the lights stopped on his shadow and began to open fire. They never did, but instead zoomed past and made for a bigger fight. Keith focused on nothing but pumping his legs and making sure to measure each breath as he ran. The gray buildings blurred past him as he ran and used his suit's power to augment his speed, trusting that Shiren was looking out for his back.

A violent punch to the gut shook Keith to the core and almost made him trip while the sound of shattering glass filled his helmet's speakers. An alarm beeped to tell him what he already knew; he had just lost his kinetic barriers. Somewhere, there was a sniper who'd just overloaded his shields with one well-placed shot. Keith knew what was coming next and resolved to do whatever needed to get the Primach out of danger. He took one last step and planted his foot before launching the Primarch as hard as he could down a dark, west facing alley, less than a second before a bullet crashed into his shoulder and exploded out the other side.

Pain blinded Keith, and the force of the shot spun him as he fell. He blinked up at the dark sky and felt only numb where his shoulder was, while hot pain stabbed his face. He rolled over and tried to crawl to the Primarch, who had landed with considerable skill. Skill not lost over her long years of inactive service.

Keith began pulling himself across the street even though he knew it was futile. A moment later, another explosion blew out a section of his thigh and the street beneath it. Keith didn't scream or yell. The suit was flooding his system with pain meds and blood coagulants to stop the bleeding and make him lucid, but he knew his body was disappearing rapidly.

The Primarch yelled something at him, but he couldn't make out exactly what. He knew there was no reason for him to struggle for himself. The Primarch was out of sight, and the sniper was too good. They would finish the job with the next shot. Keith let out a long breath and waited for death to take him.

An explosion took out a chunk of the street a foot to his left and fragments of it rained down on his helmet. He didn't quite understand as two hands grabbed his back and dragged him into an alleyway. He was rolled over and found himself staring into the fiery eyes of the Primarch. Here was the woman he knew from so long ago, harder than ever.

"The sniper missed?" was all Keith's fat tongue could get out. Sweat was pouring down his cheeks inside his helmet, and the meds the suit supplied were working to full effect.

"No thanks to you, quitter," the Primarch spat in his face. But her eyes softened as they darted to his wounds. Keith undid the left and right clamps on his helmet one handed and lifted it off slowly. Once the faceplate was gone, he noticed he had cracked it, explaining why his face was cut. The cold, night air of Drati felt wonderful against his hot skin.

"Take this road south for three blocks. Then west for two. You're looking for a repair shop. Old fashion sign above the door. Ship's in the back. Pilot named Neem is waiting for you." Keith spoke slowly and quietly with his eyes closed, savoring every moment his skin drank up the cool breeze.

Shiren looked at him with that cold stare. "Giving up on me, huh? If I had known you'd die like this, I wouldn't have wasted all those years training you."

"Thanks," he said with a smile.

She knelt down and kissed his forehead hard. He opened his eyes to see her face laced with sorrow and pain, though she was trying to hold it back. He had never seen her express so much emotion.

"Tell my brother he was right. I should have gone into politics with him."

"Brian? Mr. Grondus will never be same without you. The planets won't be the same without you. Who's going to lead us now? I mean, *really* lead us?"

Keith smiled at her and did his best to shrug. She rose from the ground and saluted him on her chest. He did the same, but opposite since he couldn't raise his right arm, and then watched her move down the street at a slow jog. She was favoring one of her legs badly, but she would make it.

Keith laid his head back and thought about calling his brother from a live feed one last time. Before the jump, he had been rather rude, and now the regret of it weighed on him. But now that he'd taken his helmet off, it was too much of a hassle to get it back on. So instead he lay in the strange warmth of his own blood and listened to the distant calls of warfare.

Several gunshots echoed through the street Keith had run through moments ago, much closer than the others, and made him draw his pistol with his left hand. It was the only weapon he had left, and if that sniper had finally come to finish the job, Keith would make sure he got a few bullets for his trouble.

More gunshots echoed in the alley, automatic fire this time, then fire from a single, high caliber weapon. Keith thought he heard muffled yelling and the identifiable sound of hard boots hitting the street. His heart raced, and his head was starting to throb. A shadow appeared in the alleyway, Keith raised his gun at it, but couldn't seem to aim correctly.

"You taking a nap, grandpa?" said a voice that sounded familiar. Keith blinked rapidly as the shadow grew closer and took on the form of a scarred battlesuit with a young human inside. "We were wondering where you got off to."

"Killer, you don't know the half of it," Keith said sleepily. Ω

Sentri

Written By
Jackson Domers

Sandrine ran into her room, slamming the door behind her and throwing herself on the bed, the imprint of her parents' embrace still visible in the delicate, golden fur of her coat.

She shrugged the tunic from her shoulders and looked at it, trying to remember the joy she had felt that morning when her father had given it to her before the ceremony, a gift well beyond anything she had ever before received, a gift that, until very recently, would have represented an entire year's work in the fields. She threw it to the floor.

It did not matter now. Nothing mattered now. The gods had made their decision. Her father would not be the next Sentri.

At the local candidate selection the previous year, the turnout had been disappointingly, though not unexpectedly, small. The luster of the Church and its traditions had faded over the past centuries, and though it was still the official religion of the people of the valley, most did little more than celebrate one or two of the major holy days, donning their finery and paying more attention to their fellows than to the priests and their dry, familiar preaching.

It had not surprised Sandrine, or anyone else in the small town, when her father had been selected as a candidate for Sentri. Their family was practically the only one that made the weekly pilgrimage to the City for worship. Most of their neighbors, when they heard that Aleander had been chosen, barely knew what it meant. A man who should have been welcomed home a hero was instead met with a few half-hearted handshakes and well more than that number of furtive glances.

The Sentri made up the Pantheon of the Church. They were nameless. Faceless. Unknowable. Though they had not always been so. They had formed the valley and its inhabitants at the dawn of time and controlled the flow of the seasons, the bounty of the harvests, and the harshness of the winter months. But they were not immortal, not permanent fixtures in the celestial firmament. Every so often, one would depart for reasons little understood by the common folk of the valley and would need to be replaced, lest some important metaphysical duties go untended.

Sandrine sat up and dangled her legs over the edge of the bed, still refusing to believe the results of the Succession Ceremony. She had been so sure that her father would be chosen, that he would join the ranks of the Sentri and watch over her, her mother, her siblings, and countless future generations of his family from above.

A Succession had not occurred in nearly a thousand years, though they had been relatively commonplace before that according to the writings of the ancients. Time had obscured these texts, and a steadily increasing number of vocal dissenters who had little interest in the Church or its teaching discounted them as little more than quaint tales of a people who did not understand their own surroundings.

How can we believe, they said, in gods that control natural processes? Is it not just as likely that water flows because that is the nature of water? That the sun shines because that is the nature of the sun? We exist, they said, and have the ability to contemplate why we exist simply because we do. Because that is how things have arisen from the natural order.

According to these doubters, to believe that mystical forces controlled the natural world was foolish. And to believe that such a mystical force would somehow wane over time and need to be replenished from the ranks of mortals was laughable. The Church, they claimed, was trying to regain its prior esteem by reviving ancient ceremonies and putting on a pageant with nothing more than a symbolic prize at its end. Perhaps the general populace of previous centuries had bought into the distraction of staged deification, but modern eyes were not so easily fooled.

Sandrine did not acknowledge the knock at her door. She raised her head only slightly when it opened, catching a glimpse of opulent azure and confirming her suspicion. She closed her eyes and pretended to sleep, hoping to avoid the conversation she knew was only moments away.

Aleander sat on the edge of the bed, shifting uncomfortably in the thick, ceremonial robes he still wore, and placed a gentle hand on his daughter's head, stroking her hair the way only a father could.

"We must trust the path that the Sentri have set before us, Sandrine," he said.

When his daughter did not respond, he joined her in silence for several minutes, unsure of how to comfort her. The public persona he had adopted of late fell away, and the verse from the Book of the Divine he had been about to cite died on his lips.

He had never been one to quote scripture before this had started, had been nothing more than a simple farmer who had chosen to follow the old ways, in large part because his own parents and their parents before them had chosen to do the same.

"I'm sorry, 'Drine," he began again, hoping that something more would come to him as he spoke. It didn't.

Sandrine said into her pillow, "Why, father? Why did they…"

The end of her question went unasked. She had been taught not to question the will of the Sentri directly. It had always seemed an unimportant rule when their work was indirect and blended into the happenings of everyday living. Now that she was faced with the direct consequences of their actions, though, the temptation was nearly too great.

"I do not understand their decision," she rephrased.

Aleander sighed and looked through the small window in the corner, seeing the sun half-hidden by the horizon, framed by the opposing, green walls of the valley. If the priests were correct in their interpretations, the Succession would occur soon, the actual transition occurring in private, away from the prying eyes of those who had gathered that morning in the center of the City for the announcement and, the critics had been half right, the pageantry.

"I'll confess, child, neither do I," his response was uncharacteristically hollow. Now that the moment was nearly here, a moment he had been preparing for with the other handful of candidates for months, he felt a brief pang of regret. Perhaps he should have done more. One more ablution. One more night of steadfast prayer. It could have made the difference, could have helped to avoid the emotions he dealt with now.

"They were supposed to choose you, father," said Sandrine, sitting up now. "They were at least supposed to choose a candidate."

"Candidacy is a great honor," said Aleander. "But there are many instances deep in the past, before the Church was fully formed, of Successions occurring without any candidates at all. The Sentri choose the most worthy, not the most popular or the most venerated. It was pure hubris to think that the clergy of today could pick the correct candidates after so many generations since the last Succession."

It was an argument borrowed from the conservatives within the Church, those who had objected to making a modern spectacle out of what should have been a solemn process, and it did little to comfort either father or daughter.

Sandrine's eyes filled with tears, and perhaps not for the first time, Aleander wished he had had it in him to abandon the ways of his family, to walk away from a faith that seemed to demand more of him than what it gave in return, a difficult truth that confronted him now more than ever before.

"But why, father?" said Sandrine, pleading now. "Why *me*?"

Aleander had known the question was coming, had thought of nothing else since the high priest had called his daughter's name that morning and shocked the gathered crowd. He had thought hard on the walk home, had remained outside of the house, watching the sun sink lower and lower until he knew he must enter and face his daughter.

His words, he knew, would be inadequate no matter what he said, but they turned out to matter even less than he had imagined. The time had come, and his final words to his daughter were swallowed by the blinding light and the deafening roar that filled the room. The first Succession in over one thousand years had begun. Ω

Deal Gone Bad

Written By
Thad Kanupp

In Chapter 2 of Deal Gone Bad, wasteland scavenger Jack solidified his friendship with young Ray, a fellow survivor who helped him out of a tight spot in an abandoned grocery store. The two managed to escape from a group of incensed bangers and set off down the road together...

Chapter 3

I told Ray the road was nothing but death. An easy, open route that made you an easy, open target. He argued that sticking to blacktop would make trouble easier to see coming. I'll admit, bangers are a lot easier to spot than the loose rocks, steep slopes, and sharp limbs waiting off-road to break your ankle or smash your head or gore your guts. But I still wasn't too keen on trotting down the highway in view of every window-lurking rifleman between where we were and where we were going. So we compromised, skirting shopping centers via fields and pastures and hitting the pavement to dodge woods and dried-out creek beds. I ended up tripping over an ambitious rock and banging my knee real good, and Ray got a good scare from a lizard half as big as he was when he went poking around in an abandoned car. So we both got a chance to say we told us so.

We made it into town right as the heat was going from unpleasant to hostile, so we decided to take a break inside a laundromat with a half-collapsed roof. I pulled a couple of water jugs from the washer I'd stashed them in the last time I came through, and Ray found the shadiest spot he could between the windows and the hole in the ceiling. I passed him a jug and slid to the floor beside him.

"Few more blocks," I said. "It's a small town. The library folks keep the immediate area pretty safe, so we should be in the clear from here on in."

"And you trust these library people?" Ray asked, wiping his mouth after a long gulp of water. "Me and Dad found a few settlements, but they weren't very friendly. They were mostly just scared, I think. Some of them ran us off."

"You had armed guards, though. People don't like risking anybody that might be a banger."

Ray shrugged. "So you trust them? Must take a lot of guys with guns to keep the bangers away."

"Much as I trust anybody. They're reliable, at least, and they've got plenty of stuff you can't get other places without a lot of work. They'll trade you for just about anything."

"But what do we have to trade?"

"Favors, mostly." I didn't bother mentioning Ray's laser pistol. It was too useful to get rid of, and I doubted he would part with it anyway. "I've done some scouting and scavenging for them before. Sometimes they'll have me go fetch something they lost or poke around a warehouse they're wondering about. Stuff they don't have time to bother with."

A few minutes later, we were strolling down the street, past the boarded and barred windows and doors of old stores. That was the library's doing. With a few exceptions, like the laundromat, they'd locked down most of the surrounding buildings. Nobody unwanted would be setting up shop in any of them without making a mess of getting in, something easy for patrols to notice.

"Is that normal?" Ray asked. We were at the post office, and a dead man was chained to its flagpole, sitting on concrete stained a nasty blood brown.

"Might be somebody they caught sneaking where they—" I started, and then I recognized him. "This is Harland. Harland the librarian."

"You know him?"

"Yeah. He kept track of the books for the library people. This isn't good." Ray reached for his gun. "Should we go back?"

"Not yet," I said. "If the library's fell, we might be in more trouble than turning around will fix." A rusted fire escape went up to the second floor of the post office, and I climbed it as stealthily as the creaking metal would allow. From the top, I could just see the library a block over, sitting on a slope that made the ground floor on one side the second floor on the other.

"Well?" Ray asked once I was back on the ground.

"Everything seems okay. The usual guards on the roof, no barricades or anything. If they were on alert, we should have run into a patrol by now. And if somebody wiped them out and set up shop themselves..." I shrugged. "Best just go in casual-like until we know what's going on. One thing first, though." Harland's pants were encased in a crust of blood, ruined by whatever injury had killed him. Looked like a blade to the thigh. But his shirt was in decent shape. I unbuttoned it and tossed it to Ray. He made a face.

"It's too big," he said.

"I know. Put it on. It'll cover your gun. We don't need to be advertising that kind of flash." He made another face, but he put the shirt on. He was short and scrawny, but Harland hadn't been a real big guy himself. The shirt was just baggy enough to make the bulge of Ray's laser and its power supply belt look like any other not-so-special heat he might be packing.

"Are you sure we're going to be safe over there?"

"Never sure about anything," I said, starting toward the library again. "But they're the only place around where we can stock up on food and supplies for this mission you're on. We can trade and scavenge here and there, but we'll be going into unfamiliar territory in a couple of days. We'll be better off with a surplus."

"Die without supplies. Die getting supplies," Ray grumbled as we walked. Quick learner.

We came at the library from the uphill side, where the second floor was at ground level. Everything seemed normal. What were once decorative planters had been sowed with food. Peppers, peanuts, squash, tomatoes, and other small, struggling status symbols. The sidewalk sloped gently up to merge into a short, concrete bridge to the building itself, spanning a little first-floor garden below. And guarding that bridge was a smirking valkyrie, slouched in an ancient folding chair.

"Jack!" she said, not moving from her chair. "Just the man I wanted to see."

"Hey, Andy." She was much the same as the last time I'd been by: lanky, a few years older than me, maybe early twenties, with blonde hair cut down to stubble on the sides and the rest knotted on top. Cut short on the right side, anyway, as everything on the left had been burned away in some accident or fight years ago. A sawed-off shotgun rested in her lap, and a short steel pipe was tucked into her belt.

"'Hey?' That's all you've got for me? Jack, I thought we were friends." She faked a hurt look that almost made me feel bad.

"I thought Harland was a friend, too."

Andy laughed. "That decrepit old tumor bag? He tried stealing from the library."

"So you chained him up and bled him out? How long was he with you?"

She shrugged. "Long enough to think he could get away with ripping us off. And you know as well as anybody that bullets aren't cheap."

My hand twinged under its bandages. "So who's keeping track of the books? Or are you just dealing food and guns now?"

"Girl named Libra," Andy said, laughing as she stood. "I swear, that's how she introduced herself. Knows books better than the old man, even if she's not as good with a gun. And who's your new friend?" She bent down in front of Ray, smiling. He leaned back an inch.

"Ray," he muttered.

Andy straightened back up and laughed. "Nice to meet you, Ray. You're in good hands with Jack, here. Probably."

"We've got a long trip ahead of us," I said. "We need a lot of food, some heat, and I want to look at some books. What do you want for it?"

"Like I said, just the man I wanted to see." She wrapped an arm around my shoulders and leaned in close. "We've got some new neighbors we don't like the looks of. You evict them, I'll set you up with a few days of food. You can stay the night here and read all you want, and I'll give you a gun when you leave."

My eyebrow popped up of its accord. "If you think I'll go get killed fighting somebody you're too scared to send your own people after, you don't know me very well."

"It's not like that, Jack." She gave me that fake-hurt look again. "Besides, what else do you have to trade? I heard somebody had a run-in with Hammer yesterday. One of his men came staggering in. Awful burns. Nothing to offer but blood and sad stories, so we sent him on his way. That hand's not looking too good."

"Then I guess we're done here." I crossed my arms, ignoring the protest of my injured hand as it tucked behind my elbow. "Come on, Ray." I started walking. Ray hesitated just a second, then fell into step beside me. He wouldn't question me right now. We'd been over that both ways. But I knew he was wondering if I was bluffing, and I wasn't too sure myself.

"Jack," Andy called from behind us. "Alright, Jack, you made your point. Name your price."

"Must be worse than I thought," I said to Ray, low enough so that Andy couldn't hear. We kept walking.

"Do we have a better choice?"

"We're probably dead either way." I admitted.

"That's nothing new. I'd rather get shot than starve."

"Ever been shot?" I waved my hurt hand at him.

He rolled his eyes. "Ever starved?"

"Now and then."

"Didn't like it, did you?"

"Didn't like getting shot, either. Are you going somewhere with this?"

"She said to name our price. That sounds like a good deal."

"Sounds like she doesn't think we're coming back is what it sounds like," I said. "We're bait, or a distraction. They ain't stupid, and they ain't weak. They can handle any bangers coming through without a fuss, so this new group must be something special. They're wanting somebody to kick the nest to see just how hard they sting, and I don't plan on being the foot. Survivors don't get involved, remember?"

We rounded a corner, out of sight of Andy, and Ray stopped in his tracks. "Survivors have contingencies, too, remember that one? We can agree to help, go take a look, and leave if we don't like what we see. They'll have to give us guns if they expect us to go kill a bunch of people, right? So we'll at least have those, and we won't be around long enough for them to come after us for taking them. They'll probably just think we got killed."

I had just stepped off the curb, onto crumbling asphalt. I kicked a piece as hard as I could, and it skittered across the street to clank against a storm drain. "They'll be watching us. For just that reason."

But Ray was right. If it came to it, we could waste an escort and be on our way. It would mean setting fire to one of my only bridges, but if the Ornel goosechase worked out, I'd never be near the library again. I stepped back up onto the sidewalk. "Fine. Let's see what we can get."

Andy was waiting when we returned. I could tell she was proud she had changed our minds, but there was relief hiding under her smirk. "I knew you wouldn't pass up a bargain," she said.

"We still might," I said. "You told me to name my price. My price is our pick of all the food and heat we can carry and a night in the library."

"Done."

"No, I'm not. A night in the library, and I get to keep anything I think's useful enough to hold onto."

Andy's triumphant smile crumbled. "Books have to stay, Jack." Her voice was low and firm.

"Keep the books. I'll rip out the pages I need."

Her jaw twitched. "Pages stay. Jack."

"Then we walk," I said, backing up. I wasn't about to turn around. "Good luck with the new neighbors. Maybe send them a cake."

"Dammit, Jack, don't do this to me. Anything but the books. The books are the only reason we're here."

"You've got smart, experienced people. They know how to farm and do repairs and whatever else you need. They don't need references." Andy just stared at me. "Maybe I won't even need to take anything. If you've got a fast scribe that can copy pictures as good as words, that might be enough. You might not even have what I'm looking for."

"Fat chance of that," she grumbled. "Fine."

"Fine." I offered my hand.

"But I'm coming with you to run these fools off." Andy said.

Without any instruction from my whiplashed brain, my hand was still hanging there after Andy shook it and went inside.

"She's coming?" Ray asked.

"Looks like it."

"Can we trust her?"

"Probably. As long as she trusts us, anyway."

"Then let's go."

The library was dark inside. The only windows were at the entrance. You could borrow a light to browse with at the desk. That's where Andy was when we came in, with an array of guns and ammo scattered across the counter beside a faded BOOK RETURN sign.

"Take your pick, boys," she said, swapping the pipe in her belt for a .45.

I picked up a rifle and looked down the sights. Andy snorted. "You been practicing since the last time I saw you shoot?" she said.

"You know me. Always learning." I laid it back on the counter and reached for a box of bullets.

"Couldn't hit a thing past the end of the barrel," she added, grinning at Ray. He smiled politely.

"Let's hope practice has paid off," I said, chambering the first round. "This hand can't work the pump on a shotty, and I'd hate to miss the guy that draws down on you."

"I'll worry about him. You just make sure you're pointed away from me."

I slung the gun over my shoulder and grabbed a revolver. "What about you, Ray? Got a preference?"

"Uh." His hand twitched toward the bulge under his shirt. "I—"

"Kids," I said shaking my head at Andy. "So indecisive." I handed him a smaller rifle. "Twenty-two. Not much kick, but not much stopping power. Aim for stuff that'll hurt."

We each had a pistol and rifle when we left, with plenty of ammo for each. Ray had his laser as well. He kept it covered, and neither of us mentioned it.

Andy had her sawed-off, too, after telling the sentry who took her place that he'd have to kill her to borrow it. And I had the big knife I'd picked up the day before. I really didn't want to get so close I had to use it.

Andy's new neighbors were a good hour's walk out of town, down the main highway. Library lookouts were posted along the route to provide an early warning in case the newcomers decided to visit. One gave us a little wave from atop a burnt-out burger joint.

"Ever wonder what beef tasted like?" I asked.

Andy shrugged. "Meat's meat. Couldn't be that much different from lizard or rat or dog."

"So you wouldn't have a problem eating me?" I asked. It was an honest question. Gotta know where people stand.

She barked out a laugh. "You wish. My stomach would crawl out and beat me to death if I tried putting it through that."

"What about you, Ray?" I asked.

"Well, maybe with the right seasoning." He leaned in, sniffed at me, and staggered back. "Nope. Not enough salt and pepper in the world to fix that, even before it ended." Andy snorted out a chuckle. Or vice versa, it was hard to tell.

"Laugh it up," I said. "I bet when we run into Andy's barbarians, they eat me first."

"My barbarians? Where'd you get barbarians?"

"You're worried enough about these people that you're trying to kick them out. I doubt it's because you think they're more civilized."

"That depends on your definition of civilized. They're well organized, and they've definitely got more sophisticated hardware. Nicer guns and stuff. But I wouldn't call slavers civilized."

I stopped. "Slavers."

"Jack—"

"You didn't say a word about slavers." My face was hot. My hands shook. Andy and Ray were right in front of me, but all I could see was my sister. She was ducked behind a concrete freeway barricade while the men she'd held off closed in. They were carrying bats and clubs. Couldn't risk the damage a bullet would do to a potential slave. She put her gun to her head. I was running, like she'd told me to. I heard a gunshot. I was running.

"Jack?" Ray shook me.

"Yeah. I'm…just give me a second." I sat down on the pavement.

"I'm sorry, Jack," Andy said.

"You're sure they're slavers?"

"Our scouts saw women and kids, a couple men, none of them armed. All inside the fence. Lots of armed guards outside. Saw a little chemistry set-up, too. They said they could smell the glass cooking a hundred yards off."

"Fence?"

Andy sighed. "They're in the old National Guard armory."

I shook my head and laid back, stretching out on the asphalt. "Somebody finally cracked the lockers."

"Maybe," Andy said. "Maybe they just thought it was a good spot."

"But if they did, you want those guns. Ray, when this all flies apart and gets me killed, you make her eat me."

"Oh, get up," Andy said. "This is just as risky for me as it is you."

"Slavers in the armory. You should have told me." I stood up.

"I was afraid you wouldn't do it."

"Well, I'm doing it now, ain't I? No wonder you were so eager to deal." Andy gave me her sweetest smile. I threw my hands up. "Well, what are we waiting for? Let's go die!" I started walking, faster than before.

Ray hurried up beside me. "Are they really that dangerous?"

"No more than anybody else with the same guns. The problem is if they decide they want to keep us instead of killing us."

"What happens then?"

"Nothing fun," I said. "Hard labor, if you're lucky. Plaything for monsters if you're not. Maybe both. Probably glass."

"What's that?"

"A drug. Feels the best kind of horrible, from what I hear. Instant addiction, good for keeping people obedient. They make it in thin sheets they can break apart and cut you with. Right into the bloodstream. You'll go down in seconds, come to hours later ready to do whatever they say to get another dose. Might actually get one, too, if you really impress them."

"Oh."

"When we met, you threatened to put a hole through my skull."

"I like you better now," he said dismissively.

"Then you won't have problem doing it if they catch me."

"You mean killing you?"

"If things go bad and you've gotta' leave without me, you peg me right between the eyes first." He nodded. I don't know if he was just putting on a brave face. The kid had grown up pretty sheltered, but he'd seen some rough stuff since leaving Packtown. He was going to see more pretty soon, I was sure.

We passed a school and a church on the way to the armory. Both had tennis courts, little fenced-in enclaves of aristocratic weeds surrounded by brown grass aspiring to their gated communities. I said as much when we reached a rec center with the same affliction.

"Yeah, real snobs," Andy said. "Get your hands on some poetry, Jack?"

"No, wait," Ray said. He ran over to the courts and slipped through the chainlink gate.

"What's he doing?" Andy asked. I shrugged, and we followed him.

"I thought I saw something," Ray said, meeting us at the gate with a smile that threatened to cut the top of his head off. He held up a double handful of blackberries.

"How in the hell?" Andy sputtered. She managed more words than me.

Ray popped a berry into his mouth. "Just have to know what to look for."

"We *do* know what to look for." Andy pushed her way into the weeds.

"Hey, don't go getting indignant on my behalf," I said, following her.

The berries weren't very big or very ripe, but they were more than worth the bloody scratches we got digging through the bushes hidden in the weeds. However Ray managed to notice them, I was glad he had. Fifteen minutes later, we'd devoured every berry we could find and were back on the road.

"We'll be getting shot at soon," I said. "It's good that we got a nice meal before the execution."

"Stop it," Andy said.

"No, think about it. We're eating blackberries, then an hour later, we're screaming and bleeding everywhere. It's surreal."

"I think we'll be okay," Ray said.

"I ever tell you you've got a weird accent? Makes 'dead' sound like 'okay.'"

"We can always quit, right?" he asked. "If there's too many of them when we get there, we can just leave. Or if one of us gets hurt, we can run away before things get worse. Retreat."

"Oh, I don't know, better ask our employer," I said, staring pointedly at Andy.

"You agreed to kick them out," she said. Her lips moved, but her jaw didn't.

"But does it have to be this trip, today?" Ray asked.

"It does if you want to get paid today. Aren't you guys going somewhere?" Ray looked at the ground. "Yeah. But we've got to be alive to get there."

"Look, I'm not thrilled with this either," she said. "You think I want to be the one expendable enough to go on what might be a suicide mission? I'm not a doctor or a mechanic. I'm good with a gun, which means I'm easy to replace and that I'm a good fit for this little excursion. So let's get it over with, okay?"

"You're the boss," I said.

The civic buildings and parking lots gave way to houses and sparse woods as we walked. We eventually veered off the road and into the trees to climb a hill that overlooked the armory, easing down to our stomachs in the dirt. Below us, surrounded by the open space of a park, was a squat, square building. Single-story offices and such clung to the side of a gym that took up the bulk of the space. There was a pair of big trucks next to a fenced-in area around back, their camouflage paint giving way to rust.

I think every scavenger in the area had made a pass at the place at least once. Inside, in a once-locked room, were still-locked gun cabinets. Only one had ever been opened. The guy who did it had gone into such a rage at finding out the weapons had trigger-locks as well, he'd smashed every one of them beyond repair. But they were good guns, everybody knew. Fully automatic.

"Looks like eight guys on the outside," Andy said, looking through her rifle's scope. "Two on the lower roof, two by the door, four more patrolling. All have rifles, probably automatic. None of them look very alert, though. Mostly watching the road." She kept watching for a few more minutes, leaving me and Ray to squint at the specks in the distance. "Definitely eight, but there might be more on the other side. One of the guys by the door keeps wandering over to the far corner. I think he's talking to someone."

"So what's the plan?" I asked.

"I think there's a blind spot to our right, mostly behind them. If we go in that way, we can get pretty close before we're noticed. Start there, run toward the building. Ray, you can cover us from one of those cars once we hit the parking lot. Get the ones on the roof first. We'll try to make for that covered walkway by the front so they can't see us from up top."

"We can watch the front," I said. "But what about other doors? I know there's a back entrance. Maybe one on the far side, too."

94

She shrugged. "One thing at a time. Ray will be watching this side if anybody comes around. We'll keep one eye on the other side until we've taken care of all the guards."

"Okay then."

"Okay then." She flipped her rifle's safety off. "Come on."

We made our way along the slope until the building blocked us from the men in front. Only three of them would have any chance of seeing us coming, unless somebody else wandered over. At the edge of the trees, Ray gagged.

"Glass," I said, trying and failing to ignore the sharp, rancid stench.

"It won't be so bad once we're upwind," Andy said. "Everybody ready? Go."

We ran. Andy's long legs pushed her ahead of me as we closed the distance. I could hear Ray's feet pounding behind me. The hundred yards to the building felt like a mile. With every step, I expected a guard to whirl around and put a slug in me. With fifty yards to go, we were still unnoticed. At forty, Ray dropped into cover behind a car. At thirty, a man on the roof turned. His head cocked to one side. His rifle started for his shoulder. Andy stopped in her tracks, aimed, fired, and was running again by the time he collapsed. Then everything exploded.

The other rooftop rifle chattered, kicking up plumes of dust to my right. Ray's .22 popped behind me. In front of me, a man sprinted around the corner of the building, gun raised. Blood fountained from the hole Andy put in his throat. I dropped to a knee as three more guards came running. My rifle kicked, and one of them grabbed her bloody stomach, screaming.

The air whined and cracked, and a sharp breeze zipped through my hair in the bullet's wake. I ran for the wall of the building. Andy was already there, dispatching the third guard with a round to the heart. The rooftop gunman stepped to the edge above her. I aimed, but Ray beat me. His bullet tore into the man's kneecap. The man jerked, yelled, and fell from the roof. His head crunched against the pavement.

"Three to go," Andy said as I pressed my back against the bricks beside her. "Either they ran inside or they're waiting for us out front. Circle around, and we'll sandwich them."

I nodded, caught my breath, and headed for the back of the building, sticking close to the wall. My stomach heaved when I got within sight of the glass-cooking setup. Bottles and jugs were arrayed across a table just inside the fence, as far from the door as possible. Some simmered on hotplates. Others were adjusted to necessary heights by stacks of boards. Tubes and hoses curled in and out of them like intestines. My eyes burned as I hurried by, shirt pulled over my nose.

Gunfire erupted from the front of the building, and I switched to a sprint. A man and woman had their backs to me when I arrived, crouched on the wide, covered sidewalk leading from the front doors. A body lay between them. The woman fired a burst at the corner Andy was using for cover. The man began to circle wide, trying to catch her with her head down. I killed him first. His partner looked over to see him die just as Andy's bullet crossed paths with mine on its way through her chest. She twisted with the double impact, falling onto her back. A flattened .45 round skittered past me on the concrete. The world was quiet.

"Watch your backstop," I hissed at Andy when we met at the entrance.

"You're fine."

"Is that all of them?" I asked, trying to remember the count.

"I think—"

Pop-pop-pop!

Ray's rifle, followed by a much closer, full-auto answer. Footsteps pounded on the metal roof above us. Andy grabbed her shotgun and followed them to the edge, turning to shoot the surprise guest from below. Instead, she staggered backwards, narrowly missing the woman that fell from the roof.

The newcomer was bleeding from two or three bullet holes. An obviously-broken arm had caught the brunt of her weight. Her busted scalp had taken the rest, matting straight black hair with blood that ran down a face twisted with pain and rage. Seeing Andy standing over her, she tried to aim her rifle. The broken arm wouldn't move right. She screamed. No words, just hate. Andy's shotgun boomed, and the woman didn't have anything left to scream with.

"Is *that* all of them?"

Andy took a few more steps out, eying the roof. "Yeah. That one must have been on the other side. Came running when she heard shots."

I waved Ray up. "Thanks for having our backs," I said when he reached us. Then I noticed the blood on his forearm.

"It's not bad," he said quickly. He wiped it on his shirt. "It hurts, but it barely nicked me. I'm okay."

"Anything?" I asked Andy. She'd gone to watch the doors.

"Nobody seems too eager to see what the ruckus was," she said. "Can't hear anything, and they covered these windows with something. I think we've got a minute to breathe and reload. Close an eye, though. It'll adjust quicker when we get inside."

I sat down and reloaded with one eye shut. The air was heavy with gunpowder and blood and voided bowels. Ray saw one of the bodies moving, feebly reaching for something that wasn't there. He took his rifle and put the guy out of his misery. Andy watched him, shrugged, and went back to loading her gun.

"Alright, everybody ready?" Andy finally asked. She got to her feet.

Ray nodded at the doors. "What if they're locked?"

Andy twisted a handle. It wasn't. "Okay, anybody has a gun and looks mean, blast them, but be careful. We don't want to hurt any slaves." She opened the door.

There was light inside. Not much, but not the darkness I expected. A lamp sat on a table in the middle of the small lobby. Cords with dim, evenly spaced bulbs were strung down halls to either side. We checked the nearest rooms and found nothing but office supplies. Every room down the first hall was empty. So was every room down the second, save a few government-issue cots. We went to the gym.

Light streamed in from the high windows above the basketball court. Posters of men rappelling from helicopters and crawling through mud covered the walls. Sign-up sheets for volleyball and basketball tournaments full of faded, dead names filled the spaces between them. Tables holding dice, dominoes, cards, and an occasional book were scattered around one half of the deserted room. Twenty cots were arranged in rows on the other half. Aside from the way we came in, there were three other doors. One went outside, one to locker rooms, and one to the armory itself. Without a word, we all drifted toward the last one.

It was dented and scarred from the first scavengers who'd tried to open it. The lock had been mangled by the one that finally cracked it, but it still latched. Andy looked at me and Ray. We readied our guns, just like we had at every other door. She grabbed the knob and jerked it open.

A boy stood in front of us, about Ray's age, looking at the rifle in his hands with complete terror. Andy jerked the gun away from him and passed it to me. The safety was on. The boy's mouth opened and shut, but he couldn't form a protest. He ran to the back of the room, past rows of open gun lockers to a huddle of people in the corner. There were three younger boys, two girls, and a pregnant woman. None of them said a word.

"It's okay," Andy said. "You're free to go. We killed the guards."

"No," the pregnant woman whispered. "Oh, no." Tears rolled down her cheeks. Two of the kids started to bawl.

Andy looked at me, then Ray, back at me, then the woman. "No, really, you're safe now. You're free. We won't hurt you, I promise." The woman was sobbing. Another kid joined in. Andy turned to me, frantic. "I don't understand. What's wrong?"

"They were already free," I said.

"What? No."

"We searched all through this place. No chains, no locked doors, nobody glassed out in a corner. The guards didn't know what they were doing. Left a blind spot, didn't manage to hit either of us with full auto from less than thirty feet. Does that sound like slavers to you?" I couldn't feel anything. Not numb, but too relieved, sick, and angry to make sense of it all.

"But…Jack, they were making *glass*."

"To trade," Ray said. He didn't look at her. Just stared at the kids in the corner.

Andy whirled on him. *"What?"*

"To trade," he said again. "Not everybody has food and books and guns to spare."

"So they scavenge—"

"Scavenge what?" he shouted. "What's left? Maybe they don't know where to look. For all you know, these people were slaves until a week ago. Maybe making glass is all they know how to do, or maybe it's all they had the material for."

"The scouts said—"

"So get better scouts!"

"Ray," I started.

"Shut up, Jack!" Ray looked at me with tear-filled eyes. "She made me kill innocent people. She made you kill innocent people." His hands were shaking.

"I didn't know," Andy said, so soft I barely heard it.

"Well, now you do," Ray snapped.

"Let's just go," she said.

"No," he growled. "You go. I'm helping these people. You go, and you bring back those scouts and show them all those slavers we killed. And then you and your scouts can bury them. And bring a stretcher or a cart or something so we can get this lady back safely. Better make it something big so you can carry all these great guns you found." He jerked away the one I was holding and shoved it into her arms. "Well?"

Andy's lip quivered. She looked at the kids, the woman. She looked at the blood spattered on the leg of her pants. "I'm sorry," she said, and left.

Ray went to the corner and crouched in front of the woman, talking softly. She nodded a few times. I waited, but he didn't say a word to me. I went back to the gym. The gun Ray'd given Andy was leaned against the wall. I put my rifle next to it and laid on a cot, trying not to think. After a while, Ray came out and sat next to me.

"Need any help?" I said.

"We all do."

"Yeah." He didn't say anything, so I added, "Bad things happen. Sometimes you're the bad thing without even meaning to be. You can't blame yourself, or me, or Andy. We're all doing our best with what we've got."

"So were these people. They were refugees, not escaped slaves. They had a little community that got hit by bangers, so they ran. Left their gardens and houses. Settled in the safest-looking place they found. One of the men had a set of lockpicks; that's how they got the guns. Another knew how to make glass, so they were doing that for some quick trading leverage. They'd been here three days. Hadn't sold a drop yet. Hadn't even seen anybody." He stretched out on his back.

"People saw the guns from a distance and thought the worst," I said. "Didn't want to take the risk. This many people this well-armed? Total fluke that they were harmless."

"People shouldn't be so paranoid."

"It keeps us alive. I know you grew up sheltered, but you had to figure that out after you left Packtown."

"Not that sheltered. We traded drugs, too. Not glass, but not harmless, either. It kept us alive."

"Huh."

"I saw my dad kill one of his best friends over me. The guy was one of our guards, the only one we had left. He wanted to go back home. Dad said no, just like he'd told the other ones. They started fighting. Just yelling, then shoving. Then I got scared and threw a rock at the guy. Hit him in the head. He pulled his gun, and Dad shot him."

I glanced back at the armory. The woman had each arm around a kid. The boy who'd had the rifle sat with his back against the doorframe, knees pulled to his chest. "Think any of them wanna' play cards?" I gestured to the tables across the room. "Get their minds off things?"

Ray shook his head. "The woman can't walk good. The kids won't leave her. And I don't think any of them want to see us right now."

I stood up. "Well, we've got time to kill until Andy gets back. Wanna' play cards? Dice? I never learned dominoes."

He sat up and rubbed at bloodshot eyes. "I can teach you."

"Yeah, you can." Ω

Nonlocal Science Fiction

nonlocalscifi.com

Thanks for reading Issue #3!

We'll be back with
our fourth issue in
December 2015!

Don't forget, we post a new FREE story
on NonlocalSciFi.com every week!

Be sure to follow us on social media
so you never miss a thing!

facebook.com
/NonlocalScifi

twitter.com
/NonlocalSciFi

www.ingramcontent.com/pod-product-compliance
Lightning Source LLC
Chambersburg PA
CBHW070224140626

46555CB00018B/1265